P9-CLA-916

# THE
# Sisters 8

## BOOK 9

THE FINAL BATTLE . . . FOR NOW

DISCARD

# THE
## Sisters 8

## BOOK 9

## THE FINAL BATTLE . . . FOR NOW

By Lauren Baratz-Logsted
With Greg Logsted & Jackie Logsted
Illustrated by Lisa K. Weber

*sandpiper*

HOUGHTON MIFFLIN HARCOURT
BOSTON • NEW YORK • 2012

Text copyright © 2012 by Lauren Baratz-Logsted,
Greg Logsted, and Jackie Logsted

Illustrations copyright © 2012 by Lisa K. Weber

All rights reserved. Published in the United States by Sandpiper, an imprint of
Houghton Mifflin Harcourt Publishing Company.

SANDPIPER and the SANDPIPER logo are trademarks of
Houghton Mifflin Harcourt Publishing Company.

For information about permission to reproduce selections from this book,
write to Permissions, Houghton Mifflin Harcourt Publishing Company,
215 Park Avenue South, New York, New York 10003.

www.hmhbooks.com

The text of this book is set in Youbee.
Book design by Carol Chu.

*Library of Congress Cataloging-in-Publication Data*
Baratz-Logsted, Lauren.
The final battle . . . for now / by Lauren Baratz-Logsted
with Greg Logsted and Jackie Logsted.
p. cm. — (The sisters eight ; bk. 9)
Summary: The Huit octuplets, each of whom has now discovered her power and
received her gift, finally learn where their parents are, but before they can attempt
a rescue they must face the Other Eights and a very scary aunt.
[1. Abandoned children—Fiction. 2. Sisters—Fiction.
3. Cousins—Fiction. 4. Magic—Fiction. 5. Humorous stories.]
I. Logsted, Greg. II. Logsted, Jackie. III. Title.
PZ7.B22966Fin 2012
[Fic]—dc22
2011003711

ISBN: 978-0-547-55441-9 paperback
ISBN: 978-0-547-55440-2 paper over board

Manufactured in the United States of America
DOC 10 9 8 7 6 5 4 3 2 1
4500364906

R0426375998

For Julia Richardson,
one last time.

Annie    Durinda    Georgia    Jackie

Marcia    Petal    Rebecca    Zinnia

# PROLOGUE

If you don't know what's going on by now, I can't help you.

Oh, very well. I'll do it just one more time. Here is the Complete and Updated List:

Annie: power — can think like an adult when necessary; gift — purple ring.

Durinda: power — can freeze people, except Zinnia; gift — green earrings.

Georgia: power — can become invisible; gift — gold compact.

Jackie: power — faster than a speeding train; gift — red cape.

Marcia: power — x-ray vision; gift — purple cloak.

Petal: power — can read people's minds; gift — silver charm bracelet.

Rebecca: power — can shoot fire from her fingertips and is really strong; gift — a locket.

Zinnia: power — can talk to cats and all other

animals as well (seriously); gift — a Christmas ornament in the shape of a snow globe.

And that's it! That's all you'll get, so don't even bother trying to beg, borrow, or steal more information from me.

See you around, or in the funny pages, whichever comes first. It's been nice knowing you.

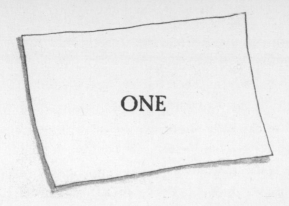

ONE

"*Daddy?*" Zinnia said.

It was August 8, 2008, the day of our official eighth birthday, and we were all still gathered outside our front door, the eight of us plus the Petes, the McGs, Will, and Mandy. A unicorn, the last in the world, according to Zinnia, had just brought Zinnia her gift, a Christmas ornament in the shape of a snow globe. Inside the snow globe was a sort of mansion that looked remarkably like our own sort of mansion, and out of the tower of the snow globe sort of mansion, our father was leaning, waving his arms wildly at us.

"Silly Daddy," Georgia said. "Now, how did he get himself inside a snow globe?"

*Silly Georgia,* we all thought. Did Daddy *look* as if he'd done this on purpose? Did Daddy *look* as if he was having fun in there? Not with all that wild arm-waving, he didn't.

"*Daddy!*" We all began shouting and wildly waving

our own arms back at him so he could see we were standing right there. *"Daddy!"*

But no matter how loudly we shouted, no matter how wildly we waved, he kept looking all around as though he couldn't see or hear us. It occurred to us then that while we could see in, he couldn't see out.

We were puzzled.

"Let's go inside and try to figure out what to do next," Annie directed. "It's tough to concentrate out here with that lion growling every five seconds."

Yes, it's true; there was a lion—more than one, actually—as well as tigers and bears and giraffes and kangaroos and pandas and strange animals we didn't even have names for filling our front lawn, plus an amazing variety of birds beating their wings overhead. The large menagerie was there because Zinnia had summoned them, having decided once and for all to prove to the rest of us that she really could talk to the animals.

We followed Annie through the front door, and so did the Petes and the McGs and Will and Mandy too, Zinnia bringing up the rear as she carefully cradled the snow globe in her hands.

Annie looked barely patient as she stood beside the open door.

"Zinnia?" Annie finally prompted.

"Hmm?" Zinnia answered vaguely without raising

her head because she was too busy staring at the tiny Daddy on the other side of the glass.

"Can you do something about this?" Annie said.

"Hmm?" Zinnia said again. "How's that?"

"All these animals!" Annie said, exasperated.

"What?" Zinnia said, raising her head at last.

"All these feathered things and beasts outside," Annie said. "Do you think you could ask your friends to leave before I shut the door? I'm worried what the neighbors will say."

\* \* \* \* \* \* \* \*

Once Zinnia had sent away the feathered things and beasts, and the door had been safely shut behind us, we gathered around the dining-room table and stared at the snow globe, trying to come up with a plan of what to do next.

"This is like something out of a fairy tale," Petal said with a shudder. "It's all so terrifying."

"Why?" Rebecca sneered. "It's just Daddy in there. It's not like it's an ogre."

"Yes, I know," Petal said, "but up until a moment ago there was a lion on our lawn, roaring its head off, plus all those other animals. There was even that unicorn, which some might have thought was a great thing to see, but I didn't. I'm terrified of the idea of things that are supposed to be imaginary turning out to be real. Why, if there's a unicorn in the world, even if it is the last one, and there's something live that's living inside a snow globe, then maybe the monster I've always heard could live under my bed is real. And if the imaginary monster under my bed is real, then where in the world will I go to hide when I get really scared?"

"So you'll just have to give up hiding," Rebecca said. "And anyway, as I believe I've already pointed out, it's just Daddy inside the snow globe. It's not like it's an ogre."

"Yes, but—"

We ignored Petal. We ignored Rebecca.

"I think this can only be seen as a good thing," Jackie said.

"How's that?" Georgia said in an unpleasant tone of voice. "Our daddy's tiny, he's trapped inside some glass thing, and we can't even reassure him that we know where he is because he can't see us."

"Yes, I know all that," Jackie said. "But for seven months and eight days, ever since we found that first note in the drawing room telling us we each needed to find our own powers and gifts before we could discover what happened to Mommy and Daddy, we've been waiting for all those things to happen. But now we have eight powers, we have eight gifts—and look! There's Daddy!"

"But he looks so skinny," Durinda said, her brow furrowed in worry, "even if he is a model. Do you think he's been eating properly?"

"It doesn't matter how skinny he is," Jackie said, for once sounding impatient. "What matters is that we can actually see him."

"It's true," Petal said, sounding cheerier at once. "Now that we can see him, Rebecca can stop saying that maybe Mommy and Daddy died — yippee!"

"After all this time," Jackie went on, "we've found him. Mommy can't be far behind."

"Well, we don't know that, do we?" Marcia said, gently taking the snow globe out of Zinnia's hands and proceeding to look carefully around the whole thing as though trying to locate a needle in a haystack. "We can only see him, not her, so there's no observable proof that she's in there too."

"But it stands to reason, doesn't it?" Jackie said. "After all, they did both disappear on the same night."

"Yes," Marcia said, "but they disappeared from different places. He disappeared when he went outside to get firewood. She disappeared when she went to the kitchen to get eggnog."

"I do know all that," Jackie said. "But the note said once we discovered our powers and gifts, we'd learn what happened to Mommy and Daddy."

"Yes," Marcia said, "*I* know all that. But the note

didn't specifically say we'd learn what happened to both of them at the same time or even that the same thing did happen to both of them. The note was only ever a note. It's not like it was some sort of official legal document with special clauses and the like."

We didn't know for sure what she was talking about. But we were sure we didn't like it.

"Oh, this is just great," Rebecca said darkly. "We now know that Daddy is . . . *somewhere*." She waved a disgusted hand in the general direction of the snow globe. "But it's still entirely possible that Mommy is—"

*"Don't say it!"* seven Eights shouted at Rebecca. We couldn't have said why, and the universe knows we'd heard her say it enough times before, but on this day—our official birthday, which was also the first time we'd seen Daddy's face live in seven months and eight days—we couldn't bear to hear her say that Mommy might be—

"I've got it!" Annie shouted gleefully. "I know where Daddy *really* is!"

???????

Seven Eights blinked.

"What are you talking about?" Rebecca said. "We can all see him. He's right there in that snow globe."

"No, he's not," Annie said, excited. "It only *looks* like he's in there. In reality, that snow globe is merely a visual representation of our house. It's like we're looking at ourselves somehow. So Daddy's not in the tower room inside the snow globe. He's actually in—"

"The tower!" Zinnia cried, clapping her hands together. But then her face fell. "But wait. How is that possible?"

"It's possible just like I just explained it is," Annie said, exasperated in spite of her excitement. "Come on, let's go get him."

"But wait," Durinda said. "Do you mean he's been in the tower for seven months and eight days and we just never noticed him all the times we went in there?"

"No, of course I don't mean that," Annie said. "But we were just away on vacation for a week or some length of time similar to that. Perhaps whoever took him in the first place deposited him in the tower while we were away and now he's locked up there, like a captive in his own home or something."

"Oh, I don't like the sound of that," Petal said.

We ignored her.

"Come on," Annie said again, "let's go free Daddy from the tower."

"But wait," Georgia said. "If Daddy was really in the real tower here, wouldn't we have noticed him waving his arms out the window to get our attention when we were all outside earlier?"

"I don't see why." Annie shrugged her shoulders. "The

only time we looked upward was when we looked at the sky during the arrival of Zinnia's feathered friends, and that was from the other direction. The rest of the time we were looking at pretty much eye level or lower, so we never would have seen him waving wildly. Plus, with all the roaring of the lions, it's not like we could have heard him screaming. If he *had* been screaming, that is. So you see . . ." Her voice trailed off.

We wanted to see, we really did, because we wanted to believe she was right. Still, it seemed like there might be a few holes in her theory.

"But—" Georgia started to say, but she never got a chance to finish.

*"No,"* Annie said firmly. "I'll listen to no more but-waits, not from Durinda or Georgia or Marcia or Petal or Rebecca or Zinnia, not even from Jackie, and she usually has only sensible things to say."

"I resent—" Georgia and Rebecca started to say in tandem, but Annie was still of a mind to cut people's speeches off prematurely.

"Forget it for now," Annie said. "All right, who's with me? Shall we go free Daddy?"

And suddenly we were *all* with her, all of us having caught the spirit of the thing.

Marcia carefully placed the snow globe on the dining-room table, and then we raced from the room and headed to the stairs. We were all the way to the foot of the stairs when—

"Wait for us!" came a shout.

Who said that?

We turned in time to see Pete running toward us, with Mrs. Pete, the McGs, Will, and Mandy not far behind him. We realized it was Pete's voice we'd heard shout after us, and we also realized we'd forgotten there were six other people in the house. Huh. Funny how things like that happened when there was so much going on.

"You shouldn't go up there alone," Pete said, already a bit winded by the time he reached us at the bottom of the stairs. "What if it's unsafe?"

"The mechanic is right," the McG said. "There should always be adult supervision."

"The principal is right," Mandy said with relief. "I couldn't agree more."

She *would* say that. She probably even thought she'd get extra credit in school somehow for saying it even though we were on summer vacation. Besides, if she hadn't said it, Petal would have.

"This is insanely exciting," Will said. "I can't believe I'm along for the ride."

"I can't believe I'm saying this," the Mr. McG said, "but I'm feeling rather excited too."

Huh. You couldn't tell from the look on his face.

"I don't think we should do this," Petal said, suddenly fearful again as she gazed up the long flight of stairs. This was Petal, so that flight of stairs must have looked like Mount Everest, with assured death waiting at the top.

"It'll be fine, dear," Mrs. Pete said, placing an arm around Petal's shoulders. "I'll stay right by your side and make sure nothing bad happens to you."

"Can you guarantee that in writing?" Petal said, looking skeptical. "Maybe do one of those contract thingies like Marcia was talking about earlier?"

Even Mrs. Pete ignored that.

"Ready, gang?" Annie said, barely able to contain both her exasperation and her excitement.

We were.

Twenty-eight feet pounded up the stairs; sixty, if you include the cats'. When we got to the top floor of the house and the tower room, Annie flung open the door.

We must say, we were rather surprised at that flinging. We'd convinced ourselves that Daddy was in the tower—or at least Annie had convinced us—and we'd further convinced ourselves that he must be being held captive there, or at least was locked in, because if he was in fact in the house, what else could explain why he didn't simply come downstairs? And yet that door—it had opened so easily, giving no resistance at all . . .

"Daddy!" we cried. "Daddy!"

No one answered.

"Mr. Huit?" Pete tried. "I've been taking very good care of your car while you've been gone."

That too failed to produce Daddy.

So we proceeded to tear the tower room apart, going over every square inch of space. We even removed everything from our costume trunk, just in case he'd somehow locked himself inside in the moments since we'd seen him waving wildly from inside the snow globe. But there was no Daddy inside the costume trunk. There was only the Daddy disguise that Annie sometimes wore when we needed to fool nosy parkers.

"He's not here," Zinnia said, a tear escaping her right eye.

"Even though I was scared to come up," Petal said, a tear escaping her left eye, "I still really wanted him to be here."

"I've got it!" Rebecca said, imitating Annie's words from earlier but sneering as she did so. "I know where Daddy *really* is!" Rebecca folded her arms across her chest and glared at Annie. "Nice work, Einstein."

"Nice work, Einstein," Marcia echoed, puzzled. "Shouldn't it be *Nice work, Sherlock*?"

\* \* \* \* \* \* \* \*

Back in the dining room, after we'd glumly trudged down there, Rebecca's patience was entirely gone.

Not that she'd ever really had any to begin with.

"Daddy's not in the house!" she shouted. "He's in this stupid snow globe and we have to get him out!"

Then, before anyone could stop her, she lifted the snow globe off the dining-room table and raised it high above her head.

*"No!"* pretty much everyone in the room shouted as Rebecca began to move to smash the snow globe on the corner of the table. Even the cats objected strenuously, in their meowing sort of way.

"Please, Rebecca," Annie said with a forced tone

of calmness, holding a steadying hand out toward Rebecca, "just put the snow globe back on the table."

"All right," Rebecca said grudgingly, "but only long enough for you to explain to me why I shouldn't do what I want to do."

"Because it's insanity!" Georgia shouted once Daddy was safely on the table again. "Even I can see that, and I'm not exactly known for my own sanity!"

"Did you see the way poor Daddy was shaking around when Rebecca raised him high?" Durinda said.

"I thought he was going to fall out of the window," Petal said, "and that would be awful. Such a long way down, even if it only looks like a few inches to us, because of course to mini-Daddy it must seem as high as the real tower does to us when we are standing on the lawn outside. I know I should hate to fall to my own death."

"He wasn't going to *die* from what I did," Rebecca scoffed.

"How do you know that?" Annie countered.

"Well, I . . . that is to say . . . er . . ." A flustered Rebecca was such a rare event, some of us were sure we'd see pigs flying soon.

"That's right," Annie said. "You don't know. All we know are, as Marcia might say, the observable facts: Daddy's in there, we're out here. But we don't know the rules of this thing. We don't know how to safely get him out."

"So I won't raise it over my head this time," Rebecca suggested, taking hold of the globe again. "That way Daddy won't fall to his death. Maybe this time I'll simply shatter it gently against the corner of the table so that he's free of his glass cage, like — "

*"No!"* pretty much everyone, plus the cats, shouted again. We realized we really were going to need to keep Rebecca away from the snow globe.

"We *don't* know how this works," Annie insisted. "Maybe there's a special atmosphere inside the snow globe. What if it's like with a fishbowl, and how if you break the fishbowl, the fish inside all die? After seven months and eight days of saying Mommy and Daddy might be dead, do you really want to be the one who finally kills Daddy?"

"No!" Rebecca was horrified. In fact, she was so horrified, she dropped Daddy.

Good thing Jackie was still faster than anyone around and was able to catch Daddy before he hit the ground. Then Jackie put him back on the table while most of us silently vowed never to pick him up again unless absolutely necessary.

"And of course," Annie went on, "even if we could be sure of getting Daddy safely out of there by smashing the glass open, we don't know if once he's free he'd be regular size again or still mini. It would be awful if he was still mini. The cats might think he was a snack."

This made sense to us. The cats weren't too careful about what they ate if they were really hungry.

"But if we can't get Daddy out here," Durinda wondered aloud, "then how will we ever be, you know, reunited again?"

"If he can't come out here," Annie said, as though it were the most reasonable thing in the world, "we'll have to get in there."

"We'll have to *what?*" Georgia said. "You're even insaner than Rebecca!"

"I don't want to become miniature," Petal said. "It's a scary enough world as it is."

"I should like to see Daddy again," Zinnia said, "sooner rather than later, but I am already the smallest one in the family. Being the smallest and being miniature might be a bit much."

"Annie may be insane about some things," Marcia said, ignoring Petal and Zinnia, like the rest of us, "but she's right about this. We need to get inside that snow globe." Marcia squinted at the base of the snow globe, a smile spreading across her face. "And I think I know just how to do it."

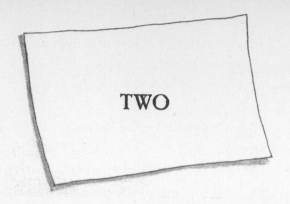

# TWO

What *was* Marcia talking about? we all wondered.

"Marcia, what *are* you talking about?" Annie demanded.

"I don't see why you're so quick to jump all over Marcia," Rebecca said to Annie. "Marcia did say you weren't insane, or at least not about this, so you do have that."

"See this at the base of the snow globe?" Marcia said, ignoring Rebecca along with the rest of us.

We looked, and suddenly we saw something we hadn't seen before. At the base of the snow globe there was a symbol that looked like the number eight lying down.

"I recognize that!" Durinda said.

"It's the infinity sign," Georgia said. "Even I recognize it!"

"I knew it," Annie said triumphantly.

"No, you didn't," Rebecca said. "You didn't even

know it was on the snow globe until Marcia pointed it out to us."

"I didn't mean that," Annie said. "I meant that I knew I was right when I insisted we all do summer workbook while we were on vacation."

We couldn't believe it. She was still going on about that?

"Thanks to me," Annie said proudly, "we all recognize what that symbol is." Then she looked less proud as she asked Marcia, "Er, so what does it have to do with anything?"

"Only this," Marcia said, getting that mad-scientist gleam in her eye we knew so well. "Remember when we first learned about the infinity sign over vacation? And then we realized it looked just like the number eight lying down?"

"Actually," Zinnia put in, "it was me who noticed that."

We ignored her. This was no time to be glomming credit for things. We expected that sort of behavior from Annie, but Zinnia?

Marcia continued as though Zinnia hadn't spoken. "And remember how we had the idea to all lie down and connect ourselves to one another to form our own lying-down-eight infinity symbol?"

"That was also my idea," Zinnia pointed out. "I was very good at ideas when we were on vacation."

More ignoring.

"Well, here's what I'm thinking," Marcia said. "If we do the same thing right now, it will magically transport us inside the snow globe."

We all stared at Marcia in wonder. Some of that wonder was positive, but some was negative.

"What are you," Rebecca said, "totally daft? That will never work!"

"How do we know until we try?" Marcia said reasonably.

"I suppose we don't," Rebecca admitted grudgingly. "But wait a second. If that's what happens, then how come it didn't happen when we did the lying-down thing while on vacation? Huh? Answer me *that*."

"Because we didn't have the snow globe then, did we?" Marcia said reasonably. "And now we do."

"I hate to say it, Marcia," Jackie said, "but that does sound a little bit far-fetched. How can you be so sure?"

Marcia shrugged. "I don't know. There are some things you learn from books and other things you just know. It's called instinct."

Jackie nodded. "I can relate to that."

"Well, I've got an instinct right now," Petal said. "I've got an instinct to go hide under the bed."

We ignored Petal, although Georgia did place a firm restraining arm around Petal's shoulders. We were going to need Petal to form our eight.

"I knew it!" Annie said. "I knew it! I knew that doing summer workbook would come in handy, and once we formed the lying-down eight, I knew it would come in handy one day too."

"Actually," Jackie pointed out, "it was Zinnia who predicted that the lying-down eight would come in handy."

That shut Annie up.

"So when do we do this thing?" Durinda asked.

"No time like the present," Annie said, having recovered quickly from being shut up. "After all, we do want to save Daddy, don't we?"

"Speaking of presents," Zinnia said, "don't you think we should open our birthday presents before we go? You know, just in case we never make it back? It's been a long time since I've opened a present . . ."

Oh, Zinnia.

"I must say," Rebecca said, "I would like to dig into that birthday cake first. It looks very enticing, what with all that frosting."

Oh, Rebecca.

"We don't have time for presents and frosting," Annie said decisively. "We need to go—"

"Excuse me," Will Simms said, interrupting Annie's decisiveness and reminding the rest of us that there were still other people in the room, "but could you explain to me what this lying-down-eight business is you're all talking about? I must say, I'm having a tough time picturing it."

"Me too," Mandy Stenko added.

"It's like this," Zinnia said, and we let her describe it since she was the one who'd come up with it in the first place. "Annie lies down on her side and curves her body a little to form one curved end of the eight. Durinda holds on to Annie's ankles and curves her hands just slightly. Georgia holds on to Durinda's ankles so she can be the line in the center. Jackie holds on to Georgia's ankles to continue the line but curves her legs a bit. Marcia grabs on to Jackie's curved legs and curves her whole body like Annie to form the other curved end of the eight. Petal grabs on to Marcia's curved ankles and curves her hands slightly. Rebecca holds on to Petal's ankles so she can be the other line in the center, crossing Georgia's line. And then I hold on to Rebecca's ankles, and then Annie grabs on to mine when I curve them slightly. And voilà! Couldn't be simpler!"

"I must say," the McG said, looking sentimental for once, "I've always worried that our teaching was somewhat useless, but the Eights have actually been learning things!"

"Well, don't get too carried away," the Mr. McG said. "Neither of us taught the Eights this stuff. They taught it to themselves."

We had a renewed appreciation for the Mr. McG in that moment. We always liked it when people gave us credit where we were due.

"Ready?" Annie said, and we all began assuming our positions on the floor.

"Wait!" Pete cried.

*Wait?* From Pete the mechanic? Really? *Wait?* At a time like this?

But wait we did. After all, Pete was asking us to do it, and it wasn't like he was just anybody. Plus, not all of us were ready to enter into the heart of darkness yet, or at least Petal wasn't. Back to our feet we rose.

"What is it, Mr. Pete?" Annie asked.

"Why, I can't let you do this alone!" he said. "What if there's real danger inside that snow globe? What if once you're in, you can't come back? No, I simply can't let you do this alone. What kind of friend would I be? What kind of loco parentis?"

Poor Pete. He looked so distraught. And now we were feeling distraught too. Except for Petal, none of us had thought of the danger. And we certainly hadn't imagined any consequences, like maybe not being able to get back out again. We'd only thought to save Daddy.

"Don't you see, Mr. Pete?" Annie said gently, taking both of Pete's large mechanic's hands in her regular-size girl's hands. "We can't take you with us, much as we might like to. For one thing, we need to make a lying-down eight, not a nine. But even if not for that, even if that would work, don't you see? We have to do this alone."

"Yes," Pete said, "I do see that. It's great to have a mum or a dad or some other adult when you need them, but it must be nice to know that, when push comes to shove, you can depend on yourselves. You can stand on your own two feet. Or sixteen feet, as the case may be." Tears welled up in his eyes. We liked to think it was because he'd miss us however long we were gone, but we also liked to think it was because he was proud of us too.

"You're always tearing up around us, Mr. Pete," Annie said, removing one of her hands from his and wiping the tears away.

"I suppose I am, aren't I, pet?" he agreed.

And then the eight of us were hugging him goodbye, hugging goodbye to Mandy and Will, the McGs and Mrs. Pete, Mrs. Pete was saying she'd take care of the cats for us, we were remembering we had cats—cats! How Zinnia begged us to take them with us, but of course Annie said no, so we each hugged each cat—Anthrax, Dandruff, Greatorex, Jaguar, Minx, Precious, Rambunctious, and Zither—which took quite a while, eight girls hugging each of eight separate cats, and then Zinnia asked one more time to open the presents and Rebecca asked once more for the frosting on the cake, and Annie said no two more times. Then we all hugged Mommy Sally and Daddy Sparky—the dressmaker's dummy and suit of armor we clothed to look like Mommy and Daddy, just in case nosy parkers peeked in our windows—and we hugged Carl the talking refrigerator and robot Betty as best as possible, considering one was a refrigerator and the other a robot, and then we hugged Pete one last time and finally got into our positions on the floor and—

The earth shook, the sky spun, and—

*Boom!*

*Bam!*

*Shazam!*

*Pow!*

*Kazowie!*

We were out of one world and into another.

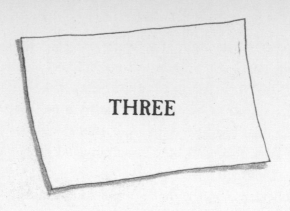

# THREE

The room we found ourselves in was quite similar to our own drawing room back home, which was a good thing, seeing so much that looked familiar, the walls made out of big slabs of gray stone, which kept things cool in summer but weren't so great in winter. Back home, the drawing room was our favorite room in the house. But there were differences here. There was no suit of armor, nor was there any grandfather clock. That, we thought, would have made Daddy happy. Daddy always hated clocks. Another thing that was different here was the fire roaring in the fireplace. Oh, we had a big fireplace in our drawing room back home too, but we'd never have built even a tiny fire in it during the hot month of August, let alone a roaring one.

"I wonder if we could be in Antarctica," Petal whispered from her position on the floor. We were all still on the floor, still in the positions in which we'd traveled here.

"What kind of idiot would make a fire in August?" Rebecca wondered loudly, not bothering to whisper.

"That would be Roberto," a boy's voice answered her.

We hastened to get to our sixteen feet and turned in the direction of the voice. A boy was seated on the floor behind a coffee table across from the fireplace. The boy had brown hair and brown eyes, not unlike Annie's, and there was something disturbingly familiar about him. We were sure we'd seen someone very much like him before, but we couldn't put our finger on it.

That boy here — that was different from our drawing room back home too.

On the table in front of the boy was a check-book — we recognized it as a checkbook because Annie used our parents' at home every month to pay the bills — and a pile of what did indeed look like bills.

"Who in the world is Roberto?" Rebecca demanded, tugging at the collar of her shirt as though she were sweltering, even though it really wasn't too bad. "And what kind of idiot is he to make a fire in August?"

We thought about pointing out to Rebecca that she'd been the kind of idiot to make a fire in July, which hardly seemed less idiotic than making one in August. In fact, Rebecca had been idiotic enough to make several fires in July, enough so that we'd had to put her in seclusion in a steel prison.

But we didn't bother pointing that out to Rebecca. We just ignored her. And so did the boy.

We began to think he might be a rather smart boy.

But then he spoiled it by talking.

"It certainly took you all long enough to get here," he said accusingly, in what we must say seemed a very judgy tone of voice.

"Ex*cuse* me?" Annie said, hands on hips.

"I said — " he started, but Marcia cut him off.

"Did you hear that?" Marcia said. "He sounds British!"

"Are you?" Jackie asked him.

"Could be," he said. "It's not for me to say."

"Are we in Britberg, then?" Petal puzzled.

"Er, no," the boy said. "I can assure you we are not that."

"What are you doing with that checkbook?" Annie demanded. "You look awfully young to be playing with a checkbook."

"I'm eight," the boy said, "and I'm not playing with it. I'm paying the bills. That's what I'm doing with this checkbook. Don't you know what people do with checkbooks?"

That shut Annie up. At least momentarily.

"Mummy usually pays the bills," the boy went on, "but she's been rather . . . *obsessed* with other things lately. I thought I'd let it go for a bit but then Peter began to fret, worrying that Bill Collector would come and get us."

"Who's Peter?" Durinda asked. She didn't need to ask about Bill Collector. In our house, we all knew about Bill Collector.

But the boy ignored her.

"Did you hear that?" Georgia whispered. "He called his mommy Mummy, which is very similar to what we call our mother. I wonder if the two could be related."

"Not being hard of hearing, I heard that," the boy said. "And to answer your question, yes, I'd say there's a good chance the two women are related. You see, I'm Andrew Ocho." He finally rose to his feet, and we could see that he was exactly as tall as Annie, which was very tall for a person who was just eight years old, and exactly seven inches taller than Zinnia. "I'm your cousin," he added.

* * * * * * * *

It took us a long moment to get over our astonishment. For quite some time now, we'd been aware there were Other Eights loose in the world, but we'd never actually pictured ourselves meeting one of them. We had so few relatives, and most of those were either crazy or absent, but now we had a cousin. A real live cousin!

We'd never had a cousin before. Well, come to think about it, apparently we'd had a cousin for eight years—we just hadn't known it!

Annie was the first to recover. Remembering her manners, she began to introduce us, but Andrew cut her off.

"I know who you all are," he said. "You see, I've been warned about you. You're Annie, the bossy one."

"I—" Annie started to object, but Andrew cut her off again.

"And you're Durinda, the motherly one. You're Georgia, the complainer."

"I—" Georgia started to object, but Andrew cut her off too.

"You're Jackie, the nice one; fast, too. You're Marcia, with the scientific mind. You're Petal, the beneath-the-bed-hider. You're Rebecca, the mean one."

"I—" Rebecca started to object, but Andrew cut her off as well.

"And finally, you're Zinnia, the one who worries about presents. I know someone else like that."

"I'll tell you one thing," Rebecca said, "getting insulted is *not* how I planned to spend my birthday."

"Oh, really?" Andrew said mildly. "Well, it's my birthday too, and this wasn't exactly my first choice either."

His birthday was the same day as ours? What were the odds?

If we gave Marcia a minute, she'd probably calculate them for us.

"This is all very nice," Annie said, "playing getting-to-know-you and having old-home week and all that, and I'm sure we all wish you a happy birthday with many happy returns. But really, we only came here to fetch our father, who we believe is in your tower."

"Oh, yes," Andrew said. "Your father. He has been making quite a racket lately."

"Is our mother with him?" Durinda asked.

"I'm afraid I'm not at liberty to say," Andrew said.

"Not at liberty . . . ?" Annie echoed, and then she shook her head. She began backing toward the door, the only exit from the room, and we followed suit. "Never mind that now. As I was saying, we're simply here to fetch our father and then we'll just be—"

"I'm afraid I can't let you do that," Andrew said.

"Can't let us?" Annie asked.

"No," Andrew said. "Mummy wouldn't like it." Then he put two fingers in his mouth and let out a loud whistle.

A great pounding came thundering toward the drawing room, accompanied by the noise of many toenails tapping against wood and marble. We turned just in time to see eight dogs enter the drawing room, filling the whole doorway and blocking our path.

Dogs!

Seven Eights reeled back in horror, all of us except Zinnia.

The dogs weren't excessively large dogs, but neither were they particularly small. They were midsize dogs, brown and white, and their faces reminded us of the joke masks our eight cats had worn to play a trick on us back on April Fools' Day. So maybe they weren't huge or especially scary-looking, but they were still dogs.

"Don't you like dogs?" Andrew said innocently.

"Not particularly," Georgia said, cringing.

"You could say we're more cat people," Petal said, and then she fainted.

Zinnia stepped up and held out her hand. The lead

dog jutted his chin forward and allowed Zinnia to give him a good scratch underneath.

"And what's your name?" she purred.

"He could tell you himself," Andrew said, "but for your sisters' benefit, he's Antibiotic. The others are Dishwater, Gewgaw, Jingle, Mysterioso, Peculiar, Riptide, and Zanzibar."

"What ridiculous names for pets," Rebecca scoffed. "Who ever heard of such outrageousness?"

We did notice that Rebecca did her scoffing at a safe distance from the dogs. While Rebecca scoffed, Zinnia commenced whispering in Antibiotic's ear. We tried to create a distraction by fake coughing and sneezing and loudly reviving Petal because we figured Zinnia was trying to worm information out of the mutt and get him to let us pass.

"I'm afraid that won't work," Andrew informed her. "Antibiotic is under strict instructions from Mummy. He'll let you scratch him until the cows come home, but he won't answer any important questions and he won't let you pass unless I tell him it's okay."

"I knew we should have brought the cats," Zinnia muttered.

We weren't quite sure what good that would have done. Our eight gray and white puffballs were amazing, but were they really any match for eight dogs? Still, we could understand why she was muttering. It was definitely turning out to be a muttering situation.

"Isn't there anything we can do to get you to let us out of this room so we can go find our father?" Annie asked.

"I could make you the best chocolate chip pancakes you've ever had in your life," Durinda offered.

Andrew shook his head.

"I could promise not to complain," Georgia offered.

Andrew shook his head.

"I could teach you some running tips," Jackie offered.

Andrew shook his head.

"I could teach you algebraic equations," Marcia offered, "as soon as I figure out what they are."

Andrew shook his head.

"I'm too scared to offer anything," Petal offered.

Andrew shook his head at the sad state of Petal, as did we all.

"I refuse to offer anything!" Rebecca said. "What—I'm supposed to make bargains with this *boy?*"

Andrew shook his head at the ridiculousness of Rebecca, as did we all.

"I still think I can talk some sense into this dog," Zinnia muttered to herself, scratching away as if she really would scratch until the cows came home.

"Isn't there anything you want from us?" Annie practically begged. "Isn't there anything we can trade so you'll let us out of this room?"

Andrew placed a thoughtful finger against his lips and tapped.

"It's been a long time since I've had a good game of chess," he said at last. "Do you play chess?"

"I've heard of it," Annie said, and then admitted, "but I can't say I've ever played the game."

"Perfect," Andrew said, his eyes lighting up. "Tell you what. We'll play one game. If you win, you get to leave this room. If I win, you stop bothering me. You let me go back to paying the bills, and you go back to wherever you came from."

"But we're not even sure how—" Durinda began to object as Annie began her own objection with "But I don't know how—" And then a lot of other partial objections were made, all one on top of the other so that none of it really made any sense.

"Take it or leave it," Andrew said firmly. "It's the only offer I'll make."

Annie held out her hand bravely for a shake. "I'll take it," she said.

"Good choice," Andrew said, that gleam still in his eye as he shook her hand.

* * * * * * * *

We wouldn't have thought that a chessboard could look menacing, but the one on the table in the corner of the room that Andrew led Annie to certainly did. Perhaps that's because so much was riding on this one game, this game Annie knew nothing about.

Annie took her seat behind the silver pieces while Andrew took his behind the gold, and Marcia whispered in Annie's ear everything she knew about chess from having read something on it in a book.

"You have eight pawns. Your pawns can move either one or two spaces on the first move," Marcia whispered. "You have two each of rooks, knights, and bishops. Your rooks move straight. Your bishops move diagonally. Your knights move in an L shape. You have one queen and one king. Your queen can move straight or diagonally but not in an L shape. Your king must be protected at all costs to keep your opponent from checkmating you. Now, you'll probably want to know about the Sicilian defense, which — "

"Pardon me," Andrew interrupted Marcia, "but are

you quite finished yet? I don't mind you giving your sister a quick tutorial, but this is getting to be a bit much."

"It's okay," Annie said to Marcia in a voice that was a weird mixture of cool-as-a-cucumber and nervous Nellie. "I think I know what I'm doing here."

Reluctantly, Marcia stepped away from Annie's ear. Then we all, including the dogs, gathered around closely, and the game began.

Andrew magnanimously gestured for Annie to go first, and she lifted the pawn that was in front of her king and moved it two squares forward. We remembered Marcia saying a pawn could be moved in the first move either one or two spaces, and we wondered why Annie had immediately opted for two, but then we figured that maybe more was better in chess. Or maybe she simply wanted to give her king extra room.

Then Andrew did something, but we didn't really notice what that was. We were still too busy puzzling over Annie's choice regarding the pawn.

Annie then moved the bishop that was next to her king diagonally three squares toward the pawn in front of Andrew's bishop, the one that was beside his king.

What *was* Annie up to? From the look on her face, we thought she might actually know what she was doing! Could she have a plan?

We were so busy wondering about that, we didn't notice
how Andrew moved.

Now Annie looked like she was growing nervous.
She cracked her knuckles, something most of us wished
she hadn't done, except for Rebecca, who began crack-
ing hers. Then Annie went in the corner and stood on
her head for a bit. Finally, she returned to the table,
ready to make her third move.

Annie took up her queen and moved it diagonally
two squares so that it stood before Andrew's king's
bishop.

We were so busy wondering whether Annie was going to go stand on her head again, we didn't notice what Andrew did.

For Annie's fourth move, which was preceded by neither head-standing nor knuckle-cracking, she pushed her queen forward and took the pawn in front of Andrew's king's bishop.

"I don't believe this!" Andrew said, moving to take Annie's queen with his king.

"Now, now," Annie said, tapping him on the back of the hand and halting his move. "Your only escape is by your king taking my queen, but you can't do that because I've protected the queen with my king's bishop. I believe this is — oh, what's the word for it — checkmate?"

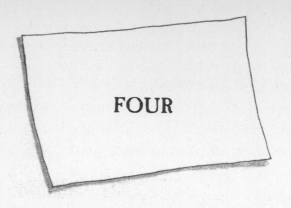

# FOUR

"I don't believe this!" Andrew said again, practically spluttering. "You beat me with the four-move checkmate. No one's beaten me with that trick since I was first learning!"

"Don't feel bad," Annie said.

"You were probably lulled into a false sense of security," Durinda said.

"Annie's been known to do that to people," Georgia said. "It's really an unfair advantage."

"She can be smart as an adult when she needs to be," Rebecca admitted.

"Well, so can I!" Andrew exclaimed. "But she'd never even played the game before!"

"Beginner's luck." Annie shrugged modestly.

"It really was," Marcia said. "I'm almost sure of it."

"Will you let us out of here now?" Petal asked Andrew. "You did promise, plus those horsy-thing knights on the chessboard are glaring daggers at me."

"You did promise," Jackie said, emphasizing the better of Petal's two points.

"Yes," Andrew said grudgingly. "Yes, I suppose I did. But you know, Mummy isn't going to like this . . ."

"Wait a second," Petal said. "It only just occurred to me. Are we actually *inside* the snow globe now?"

"It would appear so," Andrew said.

"But this is horrible!" Petal said.

"Well," Andrew said dryly, "it's not like this would have been my first choice."

"But it's awful!" Petal said. "I'm miniature now, and I'm quite certain that it is awful to be miniature. Doesn't this put me at great risk?"

"No more than it does Jackie or any of the rest of us," Annie said.

"Do I *look* much smaller to you?" Petal asked us frantically.

"Of course not," Marcia said, "because it's all relative."

"I don't even know what that means!" Petal said. "I'm miniature, so I could get stomped on by a giant, or even someone normal-size!"

"First off," Durinda said, "there's no such thing as giants."

"Or at least not that we know of," Georgia corrected.

"And second," Jackie said, "when Marcia says it's

all relative, she means that while you might be smaller in here, everything else is too."

"Which means that you're the same as you've always been," Rebecca said. "You're one inch shorter than Marcia and one inch taller than me, which I must say always does come as a shock."

"Excuse me," Zinnia said, "but could we stop all of this now and let Andrew get on with the business of letting us out of this room? I am enjoying the dogs but I would like to find Daddy sometime today."

"Come on," Andrew said. "Antibiotic, Dishwater, Gewgaw, Jingle, Mysterioso, Peculiar, Riptide, and Zanzibar—heel!"

The eight dogs immediately moved through the doorway and went to stand beside Andrew. Huh. We hadn't known dogs could all be so obedient at once like that. Our cats never behaved that way.

"Off you go, then," Andrew said to us. "Shoo."

We didn't have to be told twice. Quickly, we shooed. Annie turned back.

"Aren't you going to come with us?" she said. Suddenly, we had the impression she liked this boy, this Ocho counterpart of hers. Then we figured it was probably because she'd been able to beat him at chess.

"What were you expecting," he said, "a guided tour? Or maybe you were expecting me to lead you straight to your father? 'Fraid not. Someone has to get these bills paid or Peter will spin himself into a fear tizzy."

"Who's Peter?" Petal asked.

But Andrew ignored her.

We turned once more and were heading toward the staircase that led to the upper part of the house when we heard barking and pounding and the sound of toenails against the floor, and we saw the eight dogs race past us and position themselves at the foot of the stairs.

"What are they doing?" Annie called back to Andrew.

"Oh, that?" He yawned. "Well, I agreed to let you get out of the drawing room, but I never said the dogs would let you go upstairs. Our bargain was for one thing, not the other." He yawned again. "Goodbye for now."

And then he was gone from the doorway.

* * * * * * * *

"Well, this is a fine how-do-you-do." Durinda harrumphed.

"I don't even know what that means," Petal said.

"Durinda means," Jackie explained, "something along the lines of 'Oh, this is just great. Now what?'"

"If she meant that," Petal said, "then why didn't she

just say so?" Petal put the back of her hand to her fore-head. "Oh no," she said. "I'm feeling faint."

"What's so new about that?" Georgia said. "You're always feeling faint. Feeling faint is your regular how-do-you-do."

"Not like scared faint," Petal said. "I feel really faint. Like I haven't had enough to eat or something."

"I hate to say it," Rebecca said, putting the back of her hand to her own forehead, "but the little idiot is right. I feel faint too."

"When was the last time any of us ate anything?" Zinnia wondered.

"We stopped for a very early breakfast on the way home from our beach vacation," Marcia said precisely. "That means that we've driven in the car, experienced the beginnings of a surprise birthday party, discovered Zinnia's power, had all manner of creatures fill our lawn, met a unicorn, received Zinnia's gift, tried to figure out how to get Daddy out of the snow globe, finally figured out how to get into the snow globe, met a cousin, met eight dogs, watched Annie beat our cousin at chess, and got freed from the drawing room." She paused for breath. "So, as you can see, it's been what is known in technical circles as 'a while.'"

"It's amazing I'm still alive and haven't starved into

a little ball of nothing," Petal said, slouching against Jackie's side from the weight of the hunger.

"I knew we should have eaten our birthday cake before coming here," Rebecca said. "Or at least the frosting."

"Look," Durinda said. "This house seems very similar to our house, so I'll bet that room over there is the kitchen. Surely no one will mind if I just make us all a little snack?"

\* \* \* \* \* \* \* \*

We entered the room, half expecting to find other people in there—weren't there any people in this house besides Andrew and our father in the tower?—but the kitchen was empty.

"Oh, I was right!" Durinda said. "This kitchen is exactly where the one in our house is, and everything looks very familiar. I'm sure I can make us a good snack in here!"

Durinda crossed to the refrigerator and put her hand on the handle, but then stopped. "I wonder what its name is?" she said in a quiet voice.

"Its name?" Georgia echoed.

"Yes, its name," Durinda said. "You know, kitchen appliances can be very sensitive about things. Remem-

ber the time Carl the talking refrigerator got upset
when he realized we all thought he was a she?"

"I'm sure it doesn't have a name," Rebecca said, exasperated. "Most refrigerators don't, you know."

"Really?" Durinda raised her eyebrows. "How odd."
With a shrug, she pulled open the door. She scanned the
contents, then got out various items: a carton of eggs, a
pitcher of orange juice, some lettuce. We thought that
last thing was an odd choice. We were in the midst of
a dangerous adventure, and Durinda expected us to eat
salads?

"Is there any pink frosting in there?" Rebecca asked. "I could use some right around now."

"'Fraid not," Durinda said. "There's only this." She removed a container of something from the fridge and handed it to Rebecca along with a clean spoon she found on the counter.

Rebecca stared at the container. "*Blue* frosting? Who on earth would choose blue frosting when there's pink in the world?" But she pulled the lid off anyway, dipped the spoon in, licked, and soon looked happy enough. Or as happy as Rebecca ever looked when she wasn't actually performing evil.

"I just don't feel right about this," Durinda said. She returned to looking through the fridge. "It feels wrong to be taking food items without first having a discussion of their nutritional value and just what exactly the refrigerator thinks we should be eating."

"You're right not to feel right about it," a boy's voice said.

We turned to see a boy standing there. He was very similar to Andrew, but this one was Durinda's height.

Before we could say anything, the boy continued. "What are you doing in my kitchen?"

\* \* \* \* \* \* \* \*

Oh, this was very bad, we realized. We knew how territorial Durinda could be about our kitchen back home, only ever letting Jackie help her with things. If the boy really considered this his kitchen, what we'd done was as bad as stealing a bone from a dog. Or eight dogs.

So, rather than directly answering his question, Annie sidestepped with "Who are you?"

"I'm Drew Ocho, of course," he said. "And there's no need to introduce yourselves. I know all about the eight of you. Why, if it weren't for you, I'd never have landed KP duty in the first place."

"What's KP duty?" Petal said, hiding behind Jackie. "And will we be eating soon?"

"KP duty is an army term," Jackie explained. "KP stands for 'Kitchen Patrol,' so he obviously means that it's his duty to prepare the food around here."

"That's right," Drew said, "which I wouldn't have to do if it weren't for you."

"You've already said that once," Marcia said. "What do you mean by that?"

"Mummy used to do most of the cooking around here, but she's been preoccupied a bit these past few months, and Duddy hasn't really been around either."

"Who's Duddy?" Zinnia asked.

"That's what we call our father." Drew's eyes narrowed. "Why? What do you call yours?"

"Daddy," Zinnia said. "Like most people."

"We do believe it's the norm," Marcia added.

"No wonder your father hasn't been around much lately," Georgia said. "If our daddy were called Duddy, he'd probably hide from the world too."

"I didn't say he was—" Drew started, but Durinda cut him off.

"Wait a second," she said. "Your brother's Andrew and you're Drew. Isn't that a bit odd, two brothers named Andrew and Drew, which are practically the same name?"

"I'm not sure," Drew said, "that people named Durinda should be throwing stones. Now, would you please put the items you took back in the fridge and get out of my kitchen?"

"Fine," Durinda said, putting back the eggs. "But I don't understand why you're so possessive about your kitchen when just a minute ago you were complaining about KP duty."

"Just because a person resents something," Drew said, "doesn't mean he'd want to relinquish that something to someone else."

"Anyway," Durinda said, putting back the juice, "it's not like it's such a great kitchen anyway. Why, your refrigerator doesn't even talk."

"And yours does?" Drew blinked.

"All the time," Durinda said. "His name's Carl. He's a regular Chatty Cathy and he's in love with robot

Betty. Mommy invented both of them. Mommy is a great scientist-inventor."

"Yes," Drew said. "I've heard that about her."

Now it was our turn to blink.

"You know things about our mother?" Annie said, being the first to recover. "Is she here?"

"I'm not at liberty to say," Drew said. "I can only tell you I've heard about her and her . . . special talents. All my life, really, it's practically all I have heard about." Before we could question him further, he snapped his fingers at Rebecca, which, we can tell you, was not something that usually happened to Rebecca. "I'll take that, please," he said, at least showing a minimum of manners as he pointed at the can of blue frosting and then opened his hand.

"Fine," Rebecca said, depositing the can in his outstretched hand. Then she tossed the spoon into the can. It made a hollow thunking sound. Rebecca wiped her mouth with the back of her wrist. "I was finished with it anyway."

Drew peered into the can, but we could have told him what he'd find in there: nothing.

"Oh dear," he said. "Roberto's not going to like this."

"Who's Roberto?" Georgia asked.

But Drew ignored her. We all did, because just then

there was a thumping sound—vastly different from a thunking sound—at the kitchen window.

"Oh, look," Durinda said, opening the window. "A carrier pigeon."

The window slid shut as the pigeon hopped across the counter and landed on Durinda's outstretched finger.

"Friend of yours?" Durinda said, extending the pigeon toward Drew. "Friend of the family?"

Drew took a step back. "I've never seen that pigeon before in my life."

Durinda shrugged. "Must be here for me, then." Durinda looked all around the pigeon and located the tiny metal tube attached to one of its legs, which made sense. If the pigeon hadn't had one, it would have been just a regular pigeon, not a carrier pigeon.

Durinda removed a tiny scroll of paper from the tiny metal tube, and we gathered around to see what it said, all except Drew, who seemed oddly scared of the pigeon. The note said:

You're doing fine work here. Now challenge Drew to a cook-off. He gets very testy when anyone challenges his cooking skills, and he's bound to make a mistake.

"What does that say?" Drew asked.

"'Frost will come early this year,'" Durinda said, crumpling the note and putting it deep in her pocket. Then she opened the window again, and we watched the pigeon fly away. We figured he couldn't get very far, this being a snow globe and all. There was snow on the ground outside, which made what Durinda had said only a semi-lie.

"Brr," Durinda said, latching the window closed. "Now then." She turned back to Drew. "What do you say you and I have a cook-off?"

*  *  *  *  *  *  *  *

"What are we cooking off for?" Drew asked, pulling ingredients from cabinets. Durinda did the same. Durinda was, of course, at a disadvantage during this portion of the cook-off, since Drew knew everything he had on hand and where it was, while she did not.

"Simple," Durinda said. "If you win, my sisters and I go hungry. But if I win, meaning I make the tastier food, you let us finally eat something and be on our way, fortified."

"But who will be the judge?" Drew said.

"We'll be each other's judge," Durinda said.

"But won't we lie?" Drew objected.

"Of course we won't," Durinda said. "A person might lie about something like, oh, I don't know, the contents of a note, but no real cook would ever lie about which dish has a superior flavor, not even if something really important was on the line."

We thought she might be exaggerating just to trick Drew, but when we looked at Durinda's face, we realized something terrifying: she was telling the truth.

Did she know what she was doing?

What if Drew was the superior cook?

If that was the case, we'd never get to eat, and then we'd starve to death before we could rescue Daddy!

(We did realize that we were all starting to sound like Petal, but intense hunger can do strange things to a person's emotional state of mind, never mind seven people's.) (Wait a second. Could Petal have been in a tizzy all her life because she was intensely hungry and just needed to eat more? Nah. She was just Petal.)

"I hope you know what you're doing, Durinda," Annie said, speaking for all of us.

* * * * * * * *

"What's that thing?" Rebecca asked when Drew had finished with his first culinary creation.

"It's rack of lamb," Drew said. "Haven't you ever seen one before?"

"It looks very nice," Jackie said.

"And those little paper booties on its feet or what-ever those things are look very cute," Petal said.

"But we don't eat meat," Durinda said. "Zinnia's doing. She said the cats said we should all become pis-catarian, so you see, you'll never win with that, because none of us can eat it."

"Fine," Drew said. "Then how about this?" He banged around with some pots and pans, did some-thing to a fish, shoved it in the oven, waited, and then pulled it back out. "There! Sole amandine! You're fish-eaters—that should make you happy."

"Amandine? Made with almonds? Really?" Durinda said. "I think that's rather risky, given all the peo-ple who suffer from nut allergies these days, don't you?"

"Do any of you suffer from nut allergies?" Drew asked.

"Well, no," Durinda admitted, "but that's hardly the point. It's the principle of the thing. So, what else have you got in your culinary arsenal?"

"Hold on," Drew said, eyes narrowing. "When are *you* going to cook something in this cook-off?"

"I'm just trying to be polite," Durinda said, leaning one hip against the counter and studying her manicure coolly. "I'm letting you go first."

"Fine," Drew said, slamming down a pie plate. He did this, that, and the other thing and soon presented us with a pie that had several inches of lightly toasted frosting on top. He'd used a blowtorch to get that toasted effect. We had to admit, it was an impressive-looking pie.

"What is that?" Georgia asked.

"It's a baked Alaska," Drew said.

"What's in that frosting?" Rebecca said. "I didn't see you using any frosting from a can."

"Well, no, but—" Drew started.

"Then it can't be any good," Rebecca said, cutting him off.

"Anyway," Durinda said, "we need something substantial to eat. None of us eats dessert for a main meal, except for Rebecca, and she's already told you your baked Alaska doesn't meet her standards."

"Look here," Drew said hotly. "I've made you my three most impressive recipes—rack of lamb, sole amandine, and baked Alaska—and you haven't made a single thing. Now it's your turn." He glared at Durinda and ordered, *"Make something."*

"Very well," Durinda said, reaching into a lower cabinet and pulling out a sack of potatoes. "First," she narrated, "you take a French potato—"

"How do you know that's a French potato?" Drew demanded. "It's probably from Idaho or somewhere more usual like that."

"Well, of course it's a *French* potato," Durinda said,

as though he were the dimmest boy in all the world. "I'm about to make *French fries,* so what other kind of potato could this possibly be?"

We all looked on, our mouths watering, as Durinda did something to the potatoes that she called julienne slicing, then arranged the raw fries on a baking sheet and popped them into the oven.

"But you're not even frying them," Drew objected. "You're baking them."

"Yes, I do know that," Durinda said. "Carl the talking refrigerator says that certain oils in moderation can be a good thing but that too much oil, or the wrong oil, is bad. You'd know that if your own refrigerator could talk to you."

Drew harrumphed and then drummed his fingers on the counter as we all waited for the timer to ding.

*Ding!*

"There!" Durinda said, using an oven mitt to remove the baking sheet. "Yippee! I win!"

"What do you mean, you win?" Drew demanded. "We haven't even tasted any of the food yet!"

"Well, of course I win," Durinda said. "I already explained: we can't eat the rack of lamb at all; we can't eat the baked Alaska for a main meal; and, honestly, do you really think sole amandine can compete with a nice warm tray of French fries?"

"But—" Drew started to object.

"Here," Durinda said, popping a French fry — made with real French potatoes, we might add — into Drew's mouth, "taste one. I'm sure you'll agree, they're quite good. What do you think?"

"Yes, it is very — " Drew started to say.

"Yippee!" seven Eights shouted. "Durinda won! We can eat now!"

"No, she didn't, and no, you can't," Drew said, his face darkening with rage and frustration as his hand began to tap nervously against his leg.

Then we saw him do a thing we'd seen one of us do before. He tapped his hand against his leg three times rapidly, then he snap-pointed his finger at Annie, who froze where she was standing. Then he did the same thing to the rest of us who'd been shouting at him — Georgia, Jackie, Marcia, Petal, Rebecca, and Zinnia — and all of them froze where they stood too, except Zinnia.

"Huh," he said, looking at his finger as though it had betrayed him by not freezing Zinnia. Then he shrugged. "I suppose I should have guessed that."

He tried to freeze Zinnia again, and if most of us hadn't been frozen, we would have seen Zinnia's image stutter as though she'd been frozen for just the briefest of seconds.

Durinda looked at him with open-mouthed wonder. "You can . . . you can . . . you can do what I used to do!"

"Yes," Drew said dryly. "Handy, isn't it?"

"Why, I wish I could still do that," Durinda said, looking frustrated now. In her frustration, she tapped her hand three times rapidly against her leg as Drew shouted, "No! Don't!" And then she snap-pointed her finger at Drew.

He froze before he could shout anything else. And as he froze, Annie, Georgia, Jackie, Marcia, Petal, and Rebecca came unfrozen.

"Huh," Durinda marveled, staring at her finger as though it were a smoking gun. "If he can freeze people, and I can freeze him, he probably could have frozen me if he'd tried. So I'm both a freezer and can be frozen — who knew?" She shrugged it off. "Oh, well. Everybody hungry?"

# FIVE

We gathered around the table that was in the dining room that was in the snow globe to enjoy our meal of sole amandine, French fries, and baked Alaska. Durinda had even found juice boxes for us, although they were starfruit, not mango. We had no idea if we were eating a very late breakfast, an early lunch, or an extraordinarily early supper—we had yet to see a clock, and it was tough to keep track of time in the snow globe.

"Hey!" Marcia said, slamming down her juice box. "I just realized something. If Durinda can freeze people again, maybe we all have our powers back here. We should try to—"

Before she could get any further, Andrew entered the dining room. "Do you mind if I join you?" he asked. "I smelled all the food, and paying bills does always make one hungry."

"Why not?" Annie said magnanimously from the

head of the table, as though this were her house. "Go grab a plate and pull up a chair."

Andrew went into the kitchen and returned a moment later with a plate. "Hey!" he said. "One of you froze Drew—good show!"

Good show? He was happy we'd frozen his brother?

"It does get annoying," he explained as though reading our minds, "Drew freezing other people all the time whenever he gets upset, so it's rather nice seeing it happen to him for a change."

"Do you have any idea how long he'll stay like that?" Marcia asked.

"I haven't a clue," Andrew said. "He's never been frozen before."

"Then we'd better eat quickly," Petal said, "before he unfreezes and does something dire to us out of revenge."

Despite the threat of something dire happening, we all continued eating our food. It was nice to gain sustenance, and it was also kind of nice, the ten of us enjoying a peaceful meal together.

Wait a second. *Ten* of us? We counted—eight of us . . . plus Andrew . . .

Who was that boy sitting and eating quietly next to Georgia, and where had he come from?

* * * * * * * *

"I recognize you!" Georgia said. "You're George, that boy who was following us on the beach when we were on vacation last week!"

"That's right," Petal said. "You admitted that you might have been following me, although you said it wasn't for anything bad . . . and then you just took off running."

"That's not possible," Andrew scoffed. "You're right, his name is George, but he wasn't at the beach last week. He couldn't have been. I'm quite certain he was right here the whole time."

But from the sly smile on George's face, some of us suspected this might not be wholly true.

"George . . . George . . ." Georgia mused. "Now, where have I heard that name before? I know! We have an uncle George!"

"So do I, as it happens," George said, speaking for the first time. "He married your aunt Martha back in June. It was a shame we were unable to attend the wedding. I'm actually named for Uncle George. I suspect you are too."

"I highly doubt" — Georgia sniffed, looking offended — "that I was named for some boy relative."

We decided it was best to let Georgia think what she liked. Most of the time it was better that way.

"Too bad you couldn't go to the wedding," Durinda said. "It was a very nice wedding."

"Well," Petal said, "except for the part where Rebecca was almost thrown off the Eiffel Tower by Crazy Serena and I was the one who had to save her, it was just peachy."

"You probably would have enjoyed the wedding week and France in general more," Rebecca said, "if you hadn't spent most of the time under your bed."

"Details," Petal said.

"Why weren't you able to go to the wedding, George?" Jackie asked.

"Because Mummy said we couldn't," George said, not sounding hugely bothered by it. Considering that George was Georgia's Ocho counterpart, we were finding him to be pleasingly mild-mannered. "She said we were too busy here."

"But you did send them a nice wedding present," Zinnia remembered for us, "or at least the wrapping paper looked very pretty and the package itself was a respectable size. What did you give them? We gave them a Deluxe Perfect-Every-Time Hamburger Maker / Manicure-Pedicure Machine. It was super and duper."

To George's credit, he didn't look at Zinnia peculiarly, the way others might have done at her pronouncement.

"Um, I'm pretty sure we gave them a punch bowl," George said.

*Wow,* we thought. *How unimaginative.*

"I suppose that would make a nice present too," Zinnia said charitably.

"Everybody finished?" Durinda asked. Then, before anyone could answer, she added, "Jackie, will you help me clear the table?"

"This isn't our house," Rebecca scoffed. "We don't have to bother with all that."

"It's just good manners," Durinda said with a shrug.

Andrew and George picked up their plates, so, against our natures, we all pitched in as well.

"Oh, look," Zinnia said when we were back in the kitchen, "the rack of lamb's still here."

"And Drew is still frozen," Marcia said.

"I can't do anything about Drew," Zinnia said, "but this rack of lamb shouldn't go to waste. Even if it's not something I'd ever eat, it's already been cooked, so someone should eat it. I know — I'll feed it to the dogs!"

Antibiotic, Dishwater, Gewgaw, Jingle, Mysterioso, Peculiar, Riptide, and Zanzibar looked happy to get it. They even tried to eat the little paper booties before realizing those parts were *not* food.

"Dogs are such silly creatures," Zinnia said, giving each dog a cheery scratch under the chin. "I do love them, as I love all animals, but they're really not as bright as, say, cats."

The dogs, possibly offended by this, went back to their post guarding the stairs.

"Hey!" Zinnia called after them. "Don't go away mad!"

"Can you blame them?" Andrew said. "You just insulted their sensibilities. And what did you mean by that, anyway, that dogs aren't as bright as cats?"

"Well, they're simply not." Zinnia shrugged. "If we leave our cats alone at home for any length of time—a day, say, or even a whole week—they'll observe how much water and kibble we've left for them and then they'll ration their own food and water accordingly. No matter how long we're gone, when we return they still have something left in their bowls. It's like they know on some level, *We need to make this last until our humans come back through that door again.* Now tell me: If you tried that same thing with your dogs—leaving them alone for a week with enough food and water to last them the entire time—what do you think they'd do?"

"I don't know exactly," Andrew said, "because I've never tried that. But I suspect they'd eat all the food right away, get sick, and then starve the rest of the time."

"I rest my case," Zinnia said with a sage nod of the head. But not content to let her case rest for very long, she added, "And I'll bet you have to take them for walks regularly, so that they can—you know. Am I right?"

"Of course!" Andrew said, outraged. "They're dogs!"

"I rest my case again," Zinnia said with another sage nod. "Our cats just use the litter box, so as you can see, our cats really are superior to—"

"Fascinating as all this may be," Georgia interrupted, "it just occurred to me: Durinda was able to freeze Drew, and Marcia started to say that thing about maybe all our powers being back, but then we got distracted by Andrew joining us and all the rest of it. But maybe if I . . ."

As she let her sentence trail off, she twitched her nose twice and disappeared.

A second later, George twitched his nose twice and disappeared too.

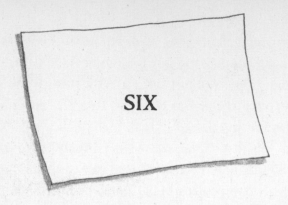

# SIX

We couldn't see Georgia anymore but we could certainly hear her shouting. The voice was coming from a direction we hadn't been in before, what we assumed to be the very front of the house.

"Quick!" invisible Georgia shouted. "I've got the front door open! And I've got an idea!"

We raced toward the sound of her voice, and Andrew raced along too, but he wisely didn't try to stop us, there being seven of us and one of him. And the dogs didn't bother following us, probably because none of their masters thought to call them, plus, we figured, maybe they didn't speak English.

We did wonder where George was. Had he tried to stop Georgia? Or maybe, even though he could make himself invisible, he couldn't actually see anyone else who was invisible?

We shrugged that off as we exited the house, finding ourselves surrounded by snow on the ground in August.

This caused us to wonder if back home, the Petes or any of the others were looking inside the snow globe, and if they were, could they see us here, as we had been able to see Daddy in the tower even though he couldn't see us back?

But then we stopped wondering as some invisible force slammed the door shut behind us and Georgia popped back into view, soon followed by George. A moment later, the kitchen window opened, and Drew's head appeared. Apparently, he'd come unfrozen.

Uh-oh.

"Hey!" he shouted. "What do you think you're doing out there?"

"Shh," George shushed him. "It appears Georgia has a plan. And I for one am curious to hear what it is."

"But—" Drew began his protest.

"No buts, Drew," Andrew said. "Now, in or out? You know Mummy won't like it if you let the house get too cold."

"Out, I suppose," Drew grumbled, swinging one leg over the sill, then the other, and then leaping down into the snow.

"I am curious," Durinda said, turning to Drew. "You're supposed to be my counterpart but you do seem grumpy all the time. Why are you like that?"

"Because I'm responsible for cooking and making sure everyone else gets fed, and yet they still sometimes complain about what I serve them," Drew said. "Mine is a thankless job. If you had my life, you'd be grumpy too."

"I do," Durinda said, then admitted, "and sometimes I am."

"Hello!" an incredibly cheery voice called from the kitchen window. "Mind if I join you?"

"Who are you?" Jackie called to the boy.

"Why, I'm Jack, of course," he said. Then, not waiting for anyone to say he could join us, he vaulted neatly over the windowsill, leaping up afterward to close the window behind him.

"So, you're Georgia, I take it?" Jack addressed Georgia in a hearty fashion. "And you're the one with the idea?"

"Brace yourself," Rebecca warned the boys. "When Georgia has an idea, it hardly ever leads to anything good."

"How can you say that?" Georgia demanded. "What about the time I had the idea not to go to the St. Patrick's Day parade at school and then saved the day when Crazy Serena had you all trapped in her dungeonlike basement?"

We had to admit, Georgia had had a good idea that time.

"Crazy Serena . . . Crazy Serena . . ." Jack, the newest Ocho to join us, mused. "Now, where have I heard that name before? I wonder: Could your Crazy Serena be our Crazy Serena?"

"Of course," Marcia said. "There can't possibly be two of them."

"Georgia," Annie said, "what was your idea?"

"Oh, right!" Georgia said, and we could have sworn we actually saw a light bulb go on over her head. "It was this: Since we can't get past those dogs on the stairs, why don't we try to get to Daddy in the tower from out here?"

We had to admit, that was a good idea.

"Excuse me," Petal piped up. "Cousin Andrew, Cousin Drew, Cousin George, Cousin Jack, do you have any bouncy boots lying around the house?"

Oh, Petal.

"What are bouncy boots?" Jack wanted to know.

"They're these amazing things," Petal said enthusiastically. "Our mother invented them. You put them on your feet and then you can bounce really high. They can be quite dangerous indoors—you know, the threat of cranium and ceiling meeting too violently—but outside, the sky's the limit, and—"

"I'm afraid we don't have any of those," Andrew said, "although they do sound like quite the thing. And, um, really bouncy."

"Well then, how about seasonal rooms?" Petal asked.

"Because if you don't have bouncy boots, I am feeling rather cold in all this snow, so I should like to go spend some time in Summer for a bit."

"Um, I'm afraid we don't have any of those things either," Andrew said.

"Drat." Petal harrumphed with a firm folding of her arms.

"Without bouncy boots," Rebecca said to Georgia, "how do you propose we get up there?" She shielded her eyes with her hand, squinting up at the tower. "It is awfully high."

"Do you have a little pink car?" Petal asked the boys.

"What would you do with a little pink car?" Annie asked Petal.

"You can't drive up the wall in one," Durinda said.

"Although sometimes at home," Rebecca said, "when Petal drives her little pink car around the house, it drives me up the wall."

"I know I can't drive up the wall with one," Petal said, peeved, "but driving one right now would relax me, especially if it had a little horn for me to beep."

"That's too bad, then," Andrew said. "We don't have one."

"How about wall-walkers?" Petal persisted. "Wall-walkers are very handy. You put them on your feet and you walk up walls. They're perfectly safe. Why, even

I'm not scared to use them, and with a pair of wall-walkers I could walk right up to that tower window."

What was with Petal coming up with all these ideas, some of which were actually rather good? It was so unlike her. Had being out in the cold opened up her brain?

"No," Andrew said, "sorry. It's a big N-O on the wall-walkers."

"Well, what good is this house anyway?" Petal harrumphed once more. "You don't have bouncy boots or Seasonal Rooms or little pink cars or wall-walkers."

"Still," Jack said, with a cheery shrug, "we kind of like it."

"There's no trees out here that we can climb to get up to that tower window," Annie said, returning us to the problem at hand.

"And while the house is made of stone," Marcia said, "the stones are too close together to allow a good toehold for climbing."

"I wonder how the cats are doing back home," Zinnia said. "Do you think they miss us when we're not there?"

"This is just great," Rebecca said. "Georgia drags us all into the cold and now we can't figure out how to achieve the thing we came out here for."

"I, for one, am going for a run," Jackie said. "I always think better when I'm running."

Jackie jogged in place for about ten seconds to warm up, and then she was off, disappearing into a tiny dot as we watched her zing around the house.

"Hey! Wait for me!" Jack yelled.

And then he jogged in place for about ten seconds before disappearing into a dot as well.

Jackie's dot was purple and Jack's was green, so it was easy enough for us to tell them apart. The first time they came back around the house, Jackie's dot was way in the lead. Well, she had gotten a nice head start. But as they zinged around a second time, we could see that the green dot was gaining on the purple dot.

"There's never any point in playing baseball with Jack," Andrew said.

"If he even just bunts the ball," Drew added, "it's always an instant home run."

"Football, basketball, tennis," George listed. "It's useless to compete when Jack's playing."

"Although he is good to have on your relay team," Andrew said.

"That may be," Annie said, "but he'll never beat Jackie."

Despite Annie's words, Jack kept gaining and gaining on Jackie, until they were running dot and dot. Since he'd caught up, we worried he might pass her. We wondered how that would make Jackie feel. We couldn't remember the last time anyone or anything had outraced her.

But that never happened.

The two of them upped their speeds until we could barely see the dots anymore as they zinged along side by side, equals, and then stopped, back among us once again.

"What we need," said Jackie, not even out of breath, "is an incredibly long rope."

"But how would we get it up there?" Georgia said. "I don't think any of us could throw a rope all that way up with any accuracy."

"I doubt we could get enough velocity from down here," Marcia said. "Gravity would be our enemy."

"Then we need someone to drop a rope out of that tower window," Jackie said, "first securing one end around a strong object in the room. With a long enough rope, it would be as good as having wall-walkers."

Eight heads swiveled to face the boys.

"Don't look at us," Jack said. "I've had more fun today than I can remember having in quite some time. After all, I don't usually get a decent race out of anyone or anything. So I'd love to help you, but I can't. Mummy would no doubt see it as aiding and abetting."

"It wouldn't end well for us," Drew added.

"How much worse can it end?" Rebecca said. "You're already on KP duty."

"Oh, it could get worse," George said, for once showing a dark side. "You don't know Mummy."

"Is she here?" Annie said. "Perhaps if we could talk to her . . ."

The boys ignored her. We all did, because that was when Jackie cupped her hands around her mouth, tilted her head up toward the tower room, and began to shout.

"Daddy!" she called at the top of her lungs. "Daddy!"

Soon we were all doing the same thing. Well, except for the boys, who no doubt would have shouted "Duddy!" instead.

"Daddy!"

*"Daddy!"*

*"DADDY!"*

At that last, the tower window flew open and a familiar head popped out. Except for a miniature ver-

sion of it glimpsed through a snow globe, it was a head we hadn't seen in seven months and eight days. The man above us rested both hands on the windowsill and leaned his upper body all the way out.

"*Daddy!*" we all shouted again, this time in incredible glee.

"*Girls!*" he shouted down at us, sounding if anything more gleeful than the eight of us combined.

Jackie shouted, "Have you got any rope up there with you?" and at the same time Daddy shouted, "How in the world did you get in here?"

But neither question got answered because just then two hands appeared—pretty hands with long red fingernails—took hold of Daddy by the forearms, yanked him back inside, and then slammed the window shut.

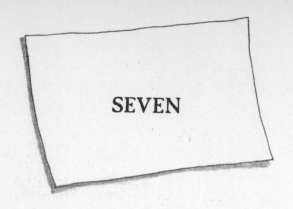

## SEVEN

*"Daddy!"* we screamed at the closed window.

What just happened?

"I wouldn't worry about it if I were you," Andrew said, "or at least not much."

"She's never killed anyone before," Drew said.

"Or at least not yet," George said.

"Not that we know of," Jack said.

"I can't help you out with the rope," a fifth boy's voice said from behind us, "but I can offer you a chance to get past the dogs."

We turned to see who had spoken.

The boy was Marcia's height.

"I'm Mark," he said. Then, singling out Marcia, he added, "And you must be Marcia."

"What do you propose?" Marcia asked by way of a response.

"Only this," Mark said. "You come downstairs with me to my basement laboratory—"

"Not the basement!" Petal shrieked in horror, cutting him off. "That's where all the spiders go to hold their meetings!"

Proving himself to be a wise Other Eight, Mark ignored Petal.

"Once we're there," Mark continued, "we'll have an invent-off, kind of like a cook-off, only with scientific inventions. The person who comes up with the best invention wins. If I win, you don't get past the dogs. But —"

"If *I* win," Marcia finished, "you call *off* the dogs."

"I like this," Rebecca said. "It's like we're going down in order to go up."

"Kind of like going south to go north," Annie said.

"Didn't we do that once on one of our vacations?" Georgia said.

"Well, I don't like this one bit," Petal said with a shudder. "I don't like that we have to go into the basement at all. But on top of that, if Marcia loses, we could be stuck down there . . . possibly forever!"

"What do you calculate your chances are of winning?" Jackie asked Marcia.

"You mean, as opposed to losing?" Marcia said.

Jackie nodded.

"Hmm," Marcia said. "Well, I'm an Eight, he's an Other Eight. I have certain talents. He, based on the evidence of his brothers, no doubt has complementary talents. That means, let's see, add twelve, subtract fourteen, add another sixteen, do a few other things . . ." She paused, considering. "I calculate my odds to be an even fifty-fifty." And now Marcia smiled. "I like those odds."

Marcia thrust out a firm hand toward Mark, who took it for a shake.

"Deal," they said at the same time.

* * * * * * * *

Down in the basement, while Marcia and Mark prepared to prepare their inventions, Petal cowered behind Durinda.

"Do your dogs even have any special powers?" Zinnia asked. "I did notice that all they seem to do is lounge around in doorways blocking people's passage."

"Why don't you ask them the next time you see them?" Rebecca suggested.

We were impressed to see that the basement laboratory was completely stocked with impressive-laboratory things.

"Do you have lab coats here?" Georgia wondered. "When doing her experiments, Marcia rather likes to look like a mad scientist."

"Actually," Rebecca admitted, "some of us like her

to look like a mad scientist too. It adds a thrilling note of insanity to the proceedings."

"Well, I don't like it," piped Petal's voice, slightly muffled by Durinda's body.

"Of course I wear a lab coat," Mark said, putting one on. Then he tossed one to Marcia. "I've even got a spare." He rooted around in a drawer and pulled out a couple more items. "And I've got protective goggles for each of us too."

Marcia put on her coat and they both put on their goggles.

"Ready?" Mark said.

Marcia nodded.

Mark did a whole bunch of things really quickly, moving all sorts of materials and potions around the lab table. While he was doing that, Marcia got a single beaker and placed it on the table in front of her.

"There!" Mark said with satisfaction as he gazed upon his invention, a cone-shaped item constructed of chicken wire and papier-mâché. There was an opening in the top of it.

"What's that supposed to be?" Marcia asked, not sounding terribly curious.

"Why, it's a homemade volcano," Mark said, as though the answer were obvious. "Now I'll create some fire," he said, rubbing two sticks together.

"Fire?" came Petal's muffled voice. "Oh no. This can't end well."

"And now," Mark said, "I'll light the volcano. Look! It's erupting just like a real volcano, with lava running down the sides and little puffs of smoke!"

"Yawn," Marcia said, not bothering to stifle her yawn. "A homemade volcano? Seriously? I think I made my first one when I was four."

"Actually," Georgia put in, "Marcia was three when she did that."

"Don't you know how to do anything more impressive?" Marcia asked Mark.

"All right then," Mark said, still game and not seeming at all bothered by the criticism. We made a note to ourselves based on what we'd observed that day: criticism could get chefs rather touchy, but scientists just seemed to find it a challenge.

Mark did another whole bunch of things, but these involved smaller items and more restrained moves than he'd used to make the volcano. Meanwhile, Marcia put some liquid that looked remarkably similar to ordinary tap water into her lone beaker.

"There!" Mark said, gleefully triumphant once more. "I just do this, this, and . . . voilà!"

At his *voilà!* tiny puffs of smoke began to explode all over the room like fireworks. They kept exploding and exploding until the entire lab was so filled with puffs of smoke, the room became as dark as a moonless night. None of us could even see our hands in front of our faces.

"What do you call this?" Marcia asked from within the puffy-smoke-filled darkness.

"I call it the Smoke Puffer," Mark said. "It's great for if you're ever in danger. You just set these off and everything goes dark—your enemies can't find you!"

As people who did indeed have some enemies, we thought this invention had some merit.

"There's just one problem," Marcia said.

"Hmm?" Mark said.

"Perhaps your enemies can't see you, but you can't see anything either," Marcia said.

"That's what the Super-Duper Night-Vision Goggles are for," Mark said.

"Oh?" Marcia said, sounding concerned for the first time. "You've invented your own set of those too, have you?"

"Well, no," Mark admitted ruefully. "But I am working on it!"

"How long is it going to be like this?" Petal fretted.

"A bit," Mark confessed.

"Oh dear," Petal said. "It's never a good idea to allow the spiders too much time in complete darkness. You never know what they might plot!"

"At least the smoke doesn't smell like anything," Jackie said.

"Yes," Durinda said, "it would be awful to be stuck in the dark with stinky smoke that could make a person cough."

"I don't know," Rebecca said darkly. "That sounds like it could be rather fun to me."

Still, despite Petal's fears and Mark's confession, the back-to-back puffs of smoke slowly began to dissolve, and soon we could see one another again.

"A homemade volcano that puffs smoke, and the Smoke Puffer," Marcia said, listing Mark's accomplishments thus far. "I'm beginning to sense a theme here. Can't you invent anything that doesn't involve smoke or explosions?"

"Seriously," Rebecca said. "Boys can be so violent."

We had to bite our tongues at Rebecca—Rebecca!—saying *that*.

"Of course I can," Mark said, finally sounding miffed. "Why, I can do all sorts of nonsmoky things that don't explode at all."

"Why don't you, then?" Marcia dared him.

Now Mark started whirling around the room like a, well, mad scientist. He poured things, mixed things, hammered and nailed things. Honestly, it was an impressive show of activity and energy.

"Excuse me?" Durinda said. "Um, Marcia?"

"Hmm?" Marcia said.

"Don't you think you should start working on your own invention now?" Durinda wondered. "Mark's already on his third, while all you've done is get out a beaker and put what looks like ordinary tap water in it."

"No," Marcia said simply.

"No?" Durinda echoed. "Then that isn't tap water? It's some amazing, fantastical clear liquid you've invented that will do all sorts of amazing and fantastical things?"

"Of course it's tap water," Marcia said. "I meant no, I shouldn't start working on my own invention just yet." Marcia smiled at Durinda. "I learned this technique from watching *you*."

"There!" Mark crowed, tossing his hammer aside.

"It looks like Mark's really outdone himself this time," Andrew said.

"It looks like one of those airport-security things you have to walk through before going on a plane," Drew said.

"I wonder if we'll ever get to fly on a plane again," George said. "It does get a little cramped in this snow globe at times, with so many people in it."

"I was caught in an avalanche once," Georgia informed George proudly.

"Excellent!" George said.

"What does it do, Mark?" Jack said with a nod toward Mark's latest invention.

"Only this," Mark said. He stepped under the airport-security-type gate, said, "Dog," and passed through to the other side.

And he was a talking dog.

"See that?" the dog said in Mark's voice. "I can still talk like me, but I can shift my shape to anything I want just by uttering a simple command."

The dog that Mark had become wagged its tail as it passed through the gate again, this time uttering, "Annie."

"It's a shape-changing machine," he said. "In fact, that's what I'm going to patent it as. The Shape-Changing Machine!"

It was really odd, Mark's voice coming out of a body that looked exactly like Annie's.

"You might want to work on that title," Marcia suggested. "I think lots of people will assume it has to do with losing weight or exercising and might therefore be disappointed with their purchase."

"I wasn't planning on selling it!" Mark was outraged. "What good would it do the Ocho family if every household had one of these? Still, I suspect you're right, and I will reconsider the name. Now watch this."

Mark, looking like Annie, walked through the gate again, this time saying, "Book."

Instantly, he was a book. A talking book.

"See?" the book said. "I can even become inanimate objects if I like."

"There's just one problem with that feature," Marcia pointed out.

"Hmm?" the book said.

"If you're an object," Marcia said, "unless you specifically command the machine to make you a walking version of the object — and can the machine even produce that level of detail for something that doesn't really exist? — you'll be stuck as that object unless someone else helps you change back."

"Oh," the book said, sounding crestfallen. "I hadn't thought of that."

"A scientist-inventor must think of things from all angles," Marcia admonished. "If no one helps you change back, you'll be a book forever."

"I like reading, but — " the book said.

"And of course," Marcia went on, "if you're a book forever, I'm pretty sure I automatically beat you at this invent-off because you'll have to forfeit."

"I suppose that's right," the book said glumly.

Poor book. It sounded so depressed.

"But I can't let that happen," Marcia said with a sigh.

"You can't?" Georgia said in shock.

"Why can't you?" Rebecca demanded. "Of course you can!"

"No." Marcia sighed again. "It wouldn't be sporting."

Then Marcia picked up the book and passed through the device. Both the book and Marcia said, "Mark," to effect the transformation, and suddenly there were two Marks.

"Oops." Marcia's voice came out of one of the Marks. "I didn't need to go overboard like that."

"But it was indeed very sporting of you," Mark said. "Thanks for that. I almost feel bad about beating you."

"Marcia," Marcia said, transforming herself as she passed through the device. Then she rounded on Mark, hands on hips. "Beat me? What do you mean, beat me? You haven't beaten me."

"Oh, but I think I have," Mark said. "I've invented three things while you've invented none."

"Oh, come on," Marcia scoffed with a very Rebecca-like scoff. "You can't count that as three, not when one's a homemade volcano and one's that ridiculous Smoke Puffer thing."

"Fine," Mark said. "Then I've only invented one thing, but it is quite an incredible thing, while you haven't invented anything."

We had to admit, the thing he'd invented was pretty incredible.

"Oh no," Petal said. "Now we'll be stuck down here forever, for Marcia can never top *that!*"

Oh, ye Petal of little faith.

"Watch *this!*" Marcia said. She took some powder, added it to her beaker of tap water, and stirred until the water turned blue.

"Oh no," Rebecca groaned. "Not the blue Kool-Aid again!"

Six others of us groaned too.

"Wait," Mark said. "Did she say Kool-Aid?"

"Of course," Marcia said. She took a sip from the beaker, licked her lips. "It's very good."

"Do you think I might have some?" Mark said.

"Sure," Marcia said, pouring some into another beaker and handing it to Mark.

Mark sipped, closed his eyes, smiled. "Okay," he said. "You win."

"What do you mean, she wins?" Andrew demanded.

"It's just Kool-Aid!" Drew said.

"It must be *some* Kool-Aid," George said.

"I wish I had some," Jack said.

"Of course she wins," Mark said. "This is a very

practical invention. I've certainly never thought of making anything like it down here. And it will come in so handy. I do get parched when working on my experiments."

Mark and Marcia clinked beakers, drank some more.

"Ahem," Annie said quietly. Then, *"Ahem,"* she added more forcefully, causing us to turn to her. "This is all very . . . *pleasant,*" she said. "But if you're going to do something practical, Marcia, then why don't you do something really practical, like using your power to see through walls to tell us what's going on. You know, *upstairs?*"

"Oh," Marcia said, light dawning. *"Oh!"*

"Exactly," Annie said. "Maybe you can even find out if Mommy's here as well as Daddy."

Marcia set her beaker down on the lab table and tilted her head back, squinting her eyes at the ceiling.

We tilted our heads too, as if we could see what she was seeing. Not that we could. It just seemed like the thing to do.

"Well," Marcia said. "I see the drawing room. There are long shadows in the room, so the sun must be setting."

"My," Jackie said, "that means we've been here for a very long time."

"At least several upon several hours," Durinda said.

"I wonder if it's time for another meal," Georgia wondered.

"I could use some more blue frosting right around now," Rebecca said.

"Too bad," Drew said sourly, "because you finished it all."

"Try to see through that room to the next story up," Annie said, "or better still, the tower."

"I'm trying," Marcia said, "but it's not as easy as I

make it seem. A house like this, with so much *stuff* in it—the images can get very confusing!"

Marcia renewed her efforts, squinting harder at the ceiling. We worried it might give her a headache.

"Oh no!" Marcia screamed, a scream that sounded very out of control for Marcia. "I see a man's legs sticking out from under a bed!"

What could that possibly mean?

Marcia whirled on the Other Eights, or at least the five of them who were with us.

"Your mummy," she screamed, "has killed our daddy!"

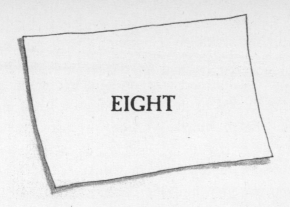

# EIGHT

Thirteen of us raced upstairs to the main floor, eight of us racing more quickly than the other five because the situation was more urgent to those eight. We raced past the open drawing-room door, past the kitchen too, arriving at the base of the stairs where the eight dogs were standing sentinel.

"Antibiotic! Dishwater! Gewgaw! Jingle! Mysterioso! Peculiar! Riptide! Zanzibar!" Mark shouted from behind us. "Out of the way!"

The eight dogs separated, four on either side of the staircase, like the Red Sea being parted by Moses.

"Honestly," Zinnia said, sounding puzzled, "these dogs don't appear to do very much."

"That's because they're *dogs!*" Rebecca shouted at her.

We raced past the dogs and up the staircase to the second story. Marcia was in the lead, her head still tilted upward, because she was the only one who could keep an eye on those feet under the bed. We raced with anticipation and fear: anticipation at the thought of seeing Daddy again, or at least his legs; and fear, because what if Marcia's vision was right and he was dead?

Achieving the landing, we were faced with a choice of doors, one on either side. Marcia squinted at each of the doors.

"This one!" Marcia cried, throwing open the door on the left.

Thank the universe it wasn't locked, for that would have presented a stumbling block, and we didn't need any more of those.

"There!" Marcia cried, pointing a finger at what we could all clearly see were two legs sticking out from beneath one of four beds in the room.

We could see something else now too.

"Those aren't Daddy's legs!" Durinda said.

"Those legs are too short for Daddy's legs," Georgia said. "He is a grown man, you know."

"And a model too," Jackie added.

"Hmm," Rebecca said, "I wonder who the dead body is?"

"What are you doing in my room?" said an angry male voice behind us.

In our minds, we went through the voices of the boys, the male cousins we'd encountered since entering the snow globe: Andrew, Drew, George, Jack, Mark. Nope, it wasn't one of those.

Slowly we turned until we came faces-to-face with a boy who was Rebecca's height.

My, but he looked angry.

"I *said*," he said, "what are you doing in my room?"

"You must be Roberto," Rebecca said, stepping forward. "I'd know you anywhere."

"Yes," Andrew said, sounding a bit nervous. "He shares this room with the other three youngest of us."

"Oh!" Zinnia said eagerly. "That's kind of like our sleeping arrangements back home: four in one bedroom, four in the other, with a connecting bathroom in between. Then at bedtime, we do the Waltons' routine, calling out to one another randomly like on the old TV show. It's great fun. Do you do the Waltons' routine too?"

"Er, no," Andrew said. He shook his head as though trying to get a fly out of his ear. "As I was starting to say, Roberto, er, doesn't usually like people entering without his permission. Roberto, these are—"

"I know who you are," Roberto said with a sneer as though he were addressing all of us, but he kept his eyes glued on Rebecca. "You're the *Other Eights*."

Rebecca reeled back as though she'd been slapped. Well, we have to admit, we all reeled back a bit. It was that shocking, hearing ourselves referred to in that fashion.

"What do you mean," Rebecca demanded, "calling us the Other Eights? We're not the Other Eights — you are!"

"Oho," Roberto said with a nasty laugh, causing us all to realize we'd never heard a human being actually say *oho* before. "I don't think so," Roberto went on. "Not from where I'm standing."

Rebecca seethed, which was never a good thing.

"You're out of order, *Eight!*" Rebecca bit off the words. "It's Petal's turn to be challenged after Marcia, not me."

"Oh dear," Petal said, "I was hoping no one would remember that and that you might just want to skip me today. I think I'll hide under this bed now."

A moment later, Petal's legs could be seen side by side with the legs that weren't Daddy's.

We ignored Petal.

"I *said,*" Rebecca said in the same nasty fashion Roberto had, "you're out of order, *Eight!*"

Then Rebecca reached through the space that separated them, made a circle of her thumb and forefinger, and then released the forefinger, flicking it against Roberto's shoulder with some degree of force.

We couldn't be absolutely certain, but we were certainly fairly certain: This was *not* a good idea.

"Oh yeah?" Roberto said, looking a peculiar mixture of outraged and thrilled as he returned the flicking favor. "Well, let's see what you've *got* . . . *Eight!*"

Rebecca and Roberto flicked each other in an increasingly fast round of flicks.

*Flick!*

*Flick!*

*Flickflickflick!*

And then they flew at each other.

Rebecca's hands locked on to Roberto's elbows in a steely grip as Roberto's hands locked on to Rebecca's elbows. They did it with such force, we fully expected to see one of them fly through a wall or something, knocked through it by the sheer will of the other.

But that didn't happen.

They remained locked in position, and yet we had the sense that something very powerful was transpiring.

"It's an impressive show of joint strength," Annie whispered, as though we were witnessing a heavyweight boxing match.

"I'm sure it must be incredibly intense," Durinda whispered.

"And yet it also really doesn't look like anything at all," Marcia said.

"Maybe if we stepped closer, we could see something actually happening," Jackie said.

"I wonder what the dogs are doing," Zinnia said. "Or the cats back home."

"Pjsdhfawoieyf," Petal said from under the bed.

"Am I the only one who finds this dull?" Georgia said.

And still, Rebecca and Roberto remained locked in frozen combat.

"All right," Annie said, "break it up, you two. It's not like this is getting any of us anywhere."

Surprisingly, Rebecca and Roberto listened to Annie and broke apart.

Rebecca glared at Roberto.

Roberto glared back at Rebecca.

Slowly, without taking their eyes off each other, they backed up until they were in opposite corners.

Then Rebecca raised her hands and pointed all ten fingers straight

out at Roberto, and Roberto did the same, pointing his fingers at Rebecca.

Uh-oh.

We'd seen this position before and we knew it couldn't possibly end well.

"Hit the deck!" Annie cried, and eleven of us did exactly just that.

We watched from the floor, amazed, as fire flew from Rebecca's fingertips toward Roberto and from Roberto's fingertips toward Rebecca.

*Hiss!*

*Crackle!*

*Zzzzzzzzzzzzzzzzzzzzzzzzzzzzz!*

It was like fireworks, like the invention of electricity, like two bolts of lightning that had somehow been released on the horizontal crashing against each other in the center.

As smoke began to fill the room from all that sizzling, it occurred to us that we were very lucky that Rebecca's and Roberto's fingers were pointed directly at the other's fingers. Otherwise, the whole house within the snow globe would have burst into flames.

"I think you can both stop that now." Annie spoke from her position on the floor.

"She's right, you know," Marcia said. "It's worse than when an irresistible force meets an immovable object. You're both irresistible forces and you're both immovable objects, so you cancel each other out."

"I'm not usually the agreeable type," Georgia said, "but suddenly I find myself agreeing. This power struggle and fire contest is hopeless."

"I'll stop if you stop," Rebecca called across the room to Roberto.

"Only if you stop first," Roberto called back.

"We'll both stop," Rebecca said. "On the count of three."

"One, two, three!" we all shouted.

Phew. That was much better. With all that sizzling, we'd barely been able to hear ourselves think.

"That got us absolutely nowhere," Durinda said.

"But it was delicious fun," Rebecca said, her eyes flashing darkly.

"And how," Roberto said.

"You know, I ate all your blue frosting," Rebecca said.

We waited for the flames to start flying again, but Roberto merely shrugged.

"So?" he said. "If it had been anyone else, I'd have to do something . . . *drastic* about it. But you, my dear cousin, are a worthy adversary."

"Thank you." Rebecca nodded her head in her version of humble. "I do love having adversaries."

Then Rebecca crossed over to one of the beds, the one that had four legs sticking out from under it, and began yanking on Petal's legs.

"Come on, Petal," Rebecca said, "it's your turn. It's time for your moment in the sun."

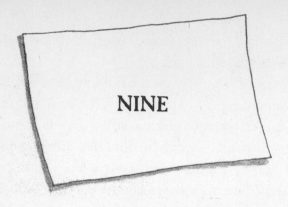

# NINE

"But I don't want a moment in the sun," Petal's muffled voice said.

"Course you do," Georgia said. "Everyone wants that."

"The cats always do," Zinnia said. "The cats love sitting in the sunlight."

"I don't think that's what Rebecca meant," Jackie gently corrected Zinnia. "She means *moment in the sun* as in 'being the center of attention.'"

"I knew what she meant," came Petal's muffled voice. "And I don't want that. I'd much rather stay under here with Peter."

Who was Peter?

Rebecca went back to yanking.

You'd think that, given Rebecca's superhuman strength, she should instantly have been able to move Petal out from under that bed. But our Petal could be a willful child when scared, and sometimes fear can overpower strength.

"Peter doesn't want to come out either," Petal's muffled voice said.

"Who's Peter?" Rebecca asked, yanking some more.

"My Ocho counterpart," Petal's muffled voice said. "He's a perfectly wonderful person. We've been comparing fears. He's much more bothered by snakes than he is by spiders and I'm the reverse but we both agree that Bill Collector is positively terrifying and we really hate standing up in front of the class and reciting things. *That* is worse than spiders, or death."

"I'm glad you've found a kindred soul," Rebecca said, causing fear in the rest of us because we weren't used to her sounding so sweet about anything. "Truly I am. But wouldn't you like to do something different for once in your life?"

"Different?" Petal's muffled voice echoed. "I don't think so. As a rule, I don't care much for different. It's too unpredictable."

"I can understand that," Rebecca soothed.

She could?

"But wouldn't it be wonderful," Rebecca went on, "for you to do something out of character for once?"

"How do you mean?" Petal's muffled voice sounded suspicious.

"Why don't you come out and I'll explain," Rebecca suggested. Then she hastened to add, "I promise, if you don't agree that my idea is good, you can go back under the bed and I won't bother you about it anymore."

"All right," Petal's muffled voice said reluctantly. "But only because you promised."

Petal slowly slid out from under the bed.

My, but her hair and face looked dusty. Still, we didn't think this was the right time to point out that she had dust bunnies and what looked like cobwebs in her hair.

"So what's your big idea?" Petal said, still seated on the floor, arms crossed defiantly.

"I thought you could use your power of reading people's thoughts," Rebecca said, "to find out things."

"But I don't like reading people's thoughts," Petal said. "They are almost always thinking bad things about me."

"And that bothers you?" Rebecca sounded surprised. "Huh. I rather relish the notion of people thinking bad things about me."

"Most people would side with Petal on this one," Durinda pointed out.

"Most normal people," Georgia added.

"So as you can see," Petal started to say, inching back toward the bed.

"Wait!" Rebecca shouted.

Petal waited, as did we all.

"I'm not suggesting," Rebecca said, "that you listen in on any of our thoughts, so you needn't worry about hearing us think bad things about you. What I want is for you to listen in on the thoughts of any people in this house who are not in this room. You know, you hear very well from a distance. You proved it that time you saved my life by reading Crazy Serena's thoughts when she was holding me hostage at the top of the Eiffel Tower. That was miles away from where you were at Uncle George and Aunt Martha's wedding, but you could hear her thoughts clearly." Rebecca paused. "You were brave that day, Petal."

"Well, I don't know about all that." Petal blushed.

"Now, look at Peter," Rebecca said. "Do you think *he* could ever do what you did?"

Petal looked at the pair of legs. "Well, perhaps not at the moment . . ."

"Even in his best moment," Rebecca said, "do you think he could save anyone's life, like you saved mine?"

Petal looked at the pair of legs. "That's very hard to say. Maybe he's never been tested like me before."

"Then think of this," Rebecca said. "Maybe, if you listen to the thoughts of the other people in this house, *maybe,* if Mommy's here you'll get to hear her too."

Petal's eyes misted over at that.

"All right," Petal said with firm resolve. "I'll do it."

As we'd learned back in June, when Petal wanted to read someone's thoughts, she did so by tilting her head to one side, as she was doing now.

"Good show," Annie whispered to Rebecca.

"Did you mean all those nice things you said about Petal?" Georgia whispered to Rebecca.

"Not hardly." Rebecca's snort was somehow quieter than usual. It was a whispered snort, if *whispered* is something that can be said of a snort. "I was merely taking one for the team."

"I heard that," Petal said, still tilting her head.

"That's because I said it out loud," Rebecca said.

"Do you think," Jackie suggested to Rebecca, "that now that you've done some good by persuading Petal to do this, you might hold off on doing any bad until after she's actually done it?"

That shut Rebecca up.

In the past seven months and eight days, we'd

grown accustomed to listening to Annie, because in the absence of our parents, she'd basically become head of the household. But we listened to Jackie too because we respected her. She was so calm and reasonable, rarely admonishing any of us for anything, that she even had a positive effect on Rebecca.

"Ooh, ooh!" Petal said, still tilting. "I think I'm getting something!"

"What? What?" We all leaned toward her.

"It sounds like," Petal said, concentrating, "*Arf. Arf, arf, arf.* I wonder what that means."

"It's the dogs," Andrew said.

"Oh, right," Petal said. "The only problem is, I don't speak dog." She turned to Zinnia. "Zinnia?"

"Is it an upset *arf* or a medium *arf*?" Zinnia wanted to know.

Petal considered this, then put her hand out and waggled it from side to side. "Medium, I'd say."

"Then it's probably," Zinnia said, "'We'd like to go for a walk sometime today,' or possibly 'Some food soon would be great,' or even 'How about a healthy scratch under the old chin?' The medium *arf*, I'm afraid, can be one of the most difficult to interpret. Not at all like *arf!* Which always means—"

"I'm sorry," Annie said, "but could we leave off worrying about dog interpretations for the time being and get back to the matter at hand?"

And then there were those times that, even though we liked Jackie's calm and reasonable way of handling things, Annie's bossiness really did make the most sense.

"Right." More head tilting from Petal. "I hear a man's thoughts," she said.

"Daddy!" we cried.

"No," Petal said. "I'm afraid it's not Daddy. This man has an accent that's different from both Daddy's *and* the Ochos we've met thus far. This accent is either Spanish or Oklahoman, one of the two."

"It sounds like it must be Duddy," Andrew said sagely.

"I have to confess," Drew said, "this is fascinating."

"It's true," Mark said. "Peter has the same power as Petal, but we never get to find out what other people are thinking from him."

"He's always been too scared to use his power," Jack said.

Petal sat up a little straighter at the favorable comparison.

"What's Duddy thinking?" George asked.

"Oh, right," Petal said, tilting once more. "He's thinking, 'Where are all those new sounds in the house coming from—unfamiliar voices yelling, feet pounding—and how do I let Queen get me wrapped up in these messes?'"

"That's so sad," Durinda said sympathetically. "He sounds very regretful."

"Try directing your mind-reading skills to another area of the house," Annie directed Petal.

Petal tilted, and soon a heavenly smile spread across her face.

What was she hearing? we wondered.

"It's Daddy," she said at last. "He's thinking, 'I do hope my girls are all still doing okay. It was so *amazing* to finally see them again earlier. And I do hope none of the others are making Petal feel like a little idiot.'" Petal wiped a tear from her eye. "Leave it to Daddy. Still worrying about my particular sensitivities, even at a time of crisis."

Secretly, we all thought that Daddy was equally worried about all of us and it was just dumb luck on Petal's part that she'd happened to stumble into his mind at the exact moment he was thinking about her. But we didn't bother pointing that out to Petal. Why destroy her moment? And we were envious of her getting to read Daddy's mind that way.

"How about Mommy?" Durinda wanted to know. "Do you hear her? Can you tell if she's even here?"

"Hmm," Petal said. "Hmm."

We waited. And waited some more.

"Oh!" Petal said. "Oh! There are a woman's thoughts roaming around the house."

"Mommy!" we cried.

"Not exactly," Petal said. "Oh, the woman's voice does sound an awful lot like Mommy's, but there's a slight edge to it."

"Uh-oh," Andrew said. "Mummy."

"The woman is thinking," Petal continued as though Andrew hadn't spoken, "'For thirty-three years, Lucy has got the best of me, but not this time.'"

"That can't be Mommy, then," Marcia said, "because Lucy is Mommy's name and she would never refer to herself in the third person. Only fabulously wealthy or really crazy people do that. I wonder what exactly is going on here."

"If you don't know what's going on by now, I can't help you."

"And there's yet *another* person's mind I can read!" Petal said triumphantly. "It's a boy's voice and it's thinking, 'If you don't know what's going on by now, I can't help you.'"

"Um, Petal," Rebecca pointed out. "You didn't read that boy's mind, because I heard those words too." Rebecca jerked a thumb over one shoulder. "And I think it came from back there."

We turned in the direction of the jerked thumb, toward the door, to see who had spoken, and we saw another boy, the smallest we'd seen yet. Well, we couldn't be sure about the one under the bed, but we could guess.

"I'm Zinn," the boy introduced himself.

"That may be," Zinnia said, stepping forward to meet him. "But you're something else too, aren't you?" Zinnia didn't give him a chance to respond before adding, "You're the note leaver."

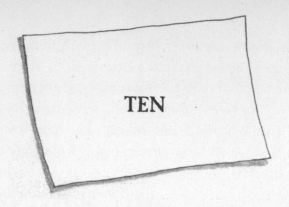

**TEN**

"What's the little one talking about," Roberto scoffed, "calling Zinn the note leaver?"

Zinnia ignored Roberto, which he probably deserved, since we didn't imagine she liked being referred to as "the little one."

"I can tell by what Jackie would call your syntax," Zinnia continued, talking to Zinn. "I'd know your syntax anywhere."

"Well," Zinn said, "I'm not usually arch, except in writing. In fact, I think you'll find I'm rather mild-spoken. After all, it's not like I go through life saying things like 'Nine down, seven to go,' which I suppose now must be 'Sixteen down and zero to go.'"

Seven of us gasped.

"It *is* the note leaver!" Marcia said, shocked.

Of all of us, Marcia had been the one most obsessed with the note leaver.

"Oh dear," Petal said. "If this Zinn is Zinnia's counterpart, then that means that he can talk to animals and summon them at will too. And *that* means that if they decide to compete, like Durinda and Drew had their cook-off and Marcia and Mark had their invent-off, they'll have something that can probably only be referred to as an animal-off, and soon this whole snow globe will be filled with lions and tigers and giraffes and other beasts, and it will be even more crowded in here." Petal paused for only the briefest of breaths before squeaking, "Time to get back under the bed!"

When there were once again four legs sticking out from under Peter's bed, Andrew approached his youngest brother.

"I don't understand, Zinn," he said. "What are they talking about, you being the note leaver?"

Annie spoke up before Zinn had a chance to answer.

"Last New Year's Eve," Annie said, "when our parents disappeared, an event I'm sure you all know something about even if you aren't saying, a note appeared behind a loose stone in our drawing room. It said we had to each discover our own power and gift before we could discover what happened to Mommy and Daddy. The note was unsigned."

"And then each month," Jackie went on, "when each of us received her power and gift, we'd receive two more notes. The notes were always very encouraging, if often arch, as Zinn says."

"I seem to remember mine being very arch." Georgia sniffed. "Some might even say insulting."

"That's only because you sent your gift back since you said it came too early," Rebecca said. "Can you blame anyone for insulting you over that?"

We ignored Georgia and Rebecca.

"Why would you *do* that, Zinn?" Drew demanded.

"Because I did want them to feel encouraged," Zinn said. "I could only imagine what it would be like if Mummy and Duddy disappeared, and I wanted them to know that if they only kept working toward their goal, they'd find a way to get in here."

"*You* told them how to get inside the snow globe?" Roberto demanded.

"How did you know how to do that?" Jack said.

"*I* don't even know that!" Mark said.

Zinn refused to answer that last series of questions, probably on the grounds that it might incriminate him.

"You sent the pigeons too," Zinnia said gently to Zinn, "didn't you?"

"*Pigeons?*" Andrew said.

"What *pigeons?*" Drew said.

"We used to get carrier pigeons coming to the

house," Durinda said. "They always had little notes attached to their legs. We thought the pigeons were friends of Daddy's, but I guess we were wrong."

"Oh, the pigeons were your father's friends," Zinn said. "But I did send them with the notes."

"Of course you did," Zinnia said, smiling at Zinn. "Who else has the power to tell animals what to do?"

"Well, *you* do, of course," Zinn said, smiling back at her.

"Oh!" Jackie said, looking very happy indeed. "So you're the person who sent all those hundreds of pigeons thundering at our house back in April, each bearing a note saying *Beware the Other Eights!*"

"Wait a second, here," Drew said. "You *warned* them? About *us?*"

"And you referred to *us* as the Other Eights?" Roberto was even more outraged than Drew. "But *they've* always been *the Other Eights!*"

"Here's what I don't understand," Zinnia said. "You sent the pigeons with the notes. I get that part. You talk to pigeons, so it makes perfect sense. And I know you wrote the other notes, because I guessed and because you admitted as much, but I don't know *how* you sent them to us. We would have seen animals delivering them inside our home, and never mind the fact that some of those notes found us outside our home."

"That's true," Jackie said. "One found us on a plane, flying over the ocean."

"And the gifts," Zinnia said, "always such nice gifts. How did you get those to us?"

"That was nothing," Zinn said. "The gifts were just a few trinkets that were lying around the house I thought you might like."

Zinnia took a deep breath. "You call a purple ring, green earrings, a gold compact, a red cape, a purple cloak, a silver charm bracelet, a locket, and a Christmas ornament in the shape of a snow globe 'just a few trinkets'?"

Leave it to Zinnia to remember everyone's present.

"I'll admit," Zinn said, "the Christmas ornament in the shape of a snow globe did present a bit of a problem."

"But we're in that snow globe right now!" Rebecca said.

"Well, yes," Zinn said. "That's true. But let me tell you, finding the last unicorn to carry it to your home this time of year was *not* easy."

"You're still not saying," Zinnia said. "How did the other presents, the ones that were not carried by a unicorn, and the other notes, the ones that were not brought by pigeons—how did you get them to us?"

Zinn remained mum, so for the longest time we did too.

Finally, when the tension in the room could go on no longer, George stepped forward.

"The reason Zinn's not answering," George said, "is that he doesn't want to rat me out. I was his accomplice. It was *me* who brought the presents that weren't brought by the unicorn. It was *me* who delivered the notes behind the loose wall in the drawing room and in the plane."

Who would have imagined that an Ocho counterpart of *Georgia* could be so *nice?*

"Why would you do that, George?" Andrew demanded.

"Because I could," George said simply. "Because it was *fun.*"

"You really were at the beach with us for a while last week," Georgia said.

"I didn't mean to get caught like that," George said, and then he winked. "But hey, at least it got me out of here."

"But *how* did you get out of here?" Georgia said.

"By making myself invisible," George said simply.

"I can make myself invisible too," Georgia said, "but I can't transport myself through space like that."

"Sure you can," George said. "Whenever I'm invisible, I can pop in and out of any place I want to."

"*No!*" Georgia's mouth dropped open.

"Yes!" George said, clearly excited for Georgia.

"You mean I could have done that when I got my power and I didn't know it?" Georgia said, still gobsmacked at the very idea.

"There were certainly times that would have come in handy," Rebecca said.

"Why don't you try it now?" George suggested.

"Oh, I don't know if I should," Georgia demurred.

*Georgia? Demurring?*

"Go on," George encouraged.

So Georgia twitched her nose twice and made herself disappear, and almost instantly we heard her voice out in the hall.

"I just thought myself here," Georgia's voice said excitedly, "and here I am!"

We're sure we were all very happy for Georgia's happiness over the new expansion of her powers, but there were still things we wanted to know and we were sure there were still things the Other Eights wanted to know too.

"How did you know we *would* each get a power at the rate of one per month?" Zinnia asked Zinn.

"Zinn," Andrew said, "how could you and George

have done all this? Weren't you worried there would be consequences?"

The word *consequences.* As Zinn failed to answer and as the sound of silence began to grow, we all reflected on the ominous nature of that one word:

*Consequences.*

Which was exactly when the earthquake came.

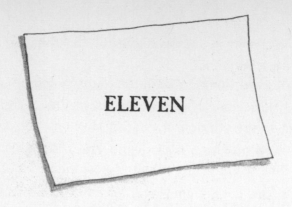

# ELEVEN

*"Earthquake!"* sixteen of us shouted.

The whole world shook back and forth; the floor kept slip-sliding beneath our feet as we tried to find solid things to hold on to to keep from falling.

"Quick!" Marcia shouted. "Everyone get to the doorway!"

"Beneath the arch of a doorway is one of the safest places to be in an earthquake," Mark added. "There's added support in that part of the structure."

We held on to one another and dragged ourselves toward the doorway as the earth continued to quiver and quake. In the doorway, the sixteen of us huddled together, wondering when this horrible shaking would stop, or *if* it would ever stop.

"I knew it!" Petal said. "I *knew* it! I knew one day the whole world would come to an end."

"I always thought the end would come with a great

big flood," Peter said, speaking for the first time. "But this is just as final."

"I'm sure the world's not ending," Durinda said.

"It's just shaking quite a bit right now," Drew said through chattering teeth.

"I hope the cats back home aren't scared," Zinnia said.

"Or the dogs right here," Zinn said. "I know the popular term is *scaredy-cat,* but dogs can be pretty scaredy too."

"If this really is the end," Rebecca said, "I hope it comes with a great big bang. I'd enjoy a great big bang."

"Yes," Roberto agreed. "It would be awful if it ended with a whimper."

"A spear would come in handy right now," Georgia said.

"I'm not sure what we'd use it for," George said, "but a spear would be delightful."

"Someone needs to take charge of this situation," Annie said.

"I think I've got a quarter in my pocket," Andrew said. "Flip you for it?"

"Look!" Jack said, pointing toward the window. "It's snowing outside!"

We looked.

It was.

Snow in August. What a curious thing.

"Wait a second," Jackie said. "*I* know what's going on. Pete is no doubt very worried that we haven't come back yet. He's probably lifted up the snow globe to see if he can see us in any of the windows."

"Who is Pete?" Mark asked.

But we never answered because just then, as abruptly as it started, the earth stopped quaking.

"Pete must have given up," Marcia said. "He's probably set us on the table again."

"Poor Pete," Durinda said. "He must be so worried. Carl's probably worried too."

"Who is Carl?" Mark asked.

"Do you think Betty's worried?" Zinnia asked.

"Not Betty," Georgia said. "I doubt she's even noticed we're gone."

"Of course," Zinnia said, "maybe it wasn't Pete at all doing that. Perhaps it was the cats playing soccer or thinking we were a multicolored ball of yarn."

"If the world's not going to end right now," Petal said, "do you think we might all move? It is very cramped here for me, being at the bottom of the heap."

"What is the meaning of this?" an adult female voice boomed at us. The voice sounded familiar and yet not.

We looked up from our huddled position and then quickly scrambled to our feet. The woman was beautiful, with dark hair and dark eyes, and the sleeveless green dress she wore looked spiffy.

"Oh, this is the best birthday present ever!" Zinnia cried, rushing forward, arms outstretched. *Mommy!*

The woman reeled back in horror.

"Do I *look* like your mother?" she said as Zinnia froze, puzzled.

"Actually," Marcia said, considering, "you look just like her. But you don't sound like her."

"You sound British," Annie said.

"And those long fingernails, painted red," Georgia said.

"Mommy always keeps her nails trimmed neat and clean," Durinda said.

"That's because Mommy's a great inventor-scientist," Jackie said.

"About those nails," Rebecca said. "Are they really yours or are they those fake press-on thingies?"

Since arriving here, we'd made a ton of noise and commotion, and yet this woman hadn't come to investigate once. Even if our mommy was working on top-secret stuff in her private office or on a new invention down in her basement lab, she would have come to investigate. Why, this woman was not only *not* Mommy but also a very poor in loco parentis.

"Oh no!" Petal cried. "If this isn't Mommy, it must be *Queen!*"

Petal nearly fainted at the horror of it all, but we had to give her credit for keeping it to *nearly*. Apparently, even Petal could see this was no time for fainting.

"That's *Aunt* Queen to you," the woman said sternly.

Aunt Queen? Oh dear. Thinking about her that way, let alone calling her that, would take some getting used to.

"I'd like to say I'm pleased to finally make your acquaintance after all these years," the woman said, "but I'm afraid I can't do that. Now, what I want to know is, how did you find this snow globe and how did you get in here?"

We kept our mouths shut tight, refusing to answer the latter because that would be giving away secret information and refusing to answer the former because that would mean ratting out Zinn. And we couldn't do that. Why, if not for Zinn, we'd never have had even a chance of finding our parents.

"It figures," the woman said, "that Lucy's children would be close-mouthed about things."

"Don't you dare talk about our mother that way," Annie said, growing bold as only Annie could. "I'm not even sure what you mean by that, but I'm sure it can't be anything good. And tell me, why have you taken our parents? We know you have Daddy here — we have seen him — and now I'm certain Mommy must be here too."

"It's Lucy's own fault," the woman said. "If she wasn't always trying to one-up me on everything just like when we were children, she'd have never gotten herself into this situation in the first place."

"One-up you?" Annie echoed.

"*One-up* you?" Rebecca shrilled. "Are you seriously going to stand there and tell me this all has to do with some stupid sibling rivalry?"

Of all of us, Rebecca would know about stupid sibling rivalry. But then, in some ways, we all did.

"I don't have to stand here and tell you anything," the woman, *our aunt,* said with a harrumph. "But I will stand here and tell you this: Now that you've all found your way in here, I'm not going to let you leave."

"Oh no," a man's voice said, a voice that had a distinctly Spanish accent, not at all Oklahoman.

We studied the man who'd appeared by Queen's side. He was tall, too thin, with curly black hair and a very tired look about him.

"Meet your uncle Joe," Andrew said to us, "the man we call Duddy."

"Oh no, Queen," Uncle Joe went on. "I will not let you do this. It's been hard enough having your sister and your brother-in-law here for all these months. That man may be a model, but he eats like a horse. And now you expect me to provide for eight more? This I cannot do."

"But Joe," Queen wheedled, placing her hands on his shoulders. "We can't let them go. It's bad enough that *I* know Lucy has one-upped me yet again. I simply can't let the rest of the world find out."

"What's the big deal?" Annie demanded. "What is it that you think our mother has one-upped you on?"

But Queen never answered because just then we heard the sound of a shout — it was *Mommy!* — followed by a small cry.

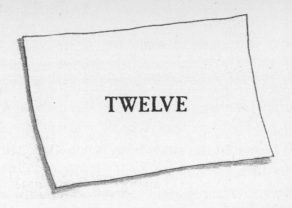

# TWELVE

We raced toward the sound of the shout and the cry, which had come from higher up in the house. We pushed past Queen, heedless of what she might try to do. If the dogs had been in our path, we'd have been heedless of any danger from them too. If all our enemies had been in our path — and we did have enemies — they couldn't have stopped us. All we knew was that Mommy was in trouble. We *had* to get to her.

We pounded up the staircase toward the tower, and as we pounded, we were filled with both excitement and fear: excitement at the prospect of finally seeing Mommy again — Mommy! — and fear because of that shout and that small cry.

The door to the tower room was shut but that presented no barrier to us. We flung it open, unsure what we would find on the other side, and then quickly ran in and shut the door behind us.

What we found was Mommy in a bed, a bundle of something in her arms, with Daddy standing over Mommy and the bundle, a great smile on his face.

"Girls!" Mommy and Daddy shouted when they saw us.

We rushed to the side of the bed, and Daddy threw open his arms and hugged us all tightly. We would have loved to hug Mommy right away, but we were worried she was sick because she was in bed and there was that bundle in her arms between us.

"How did you ever find us and get in here?" Daddy said.

We didn't like to ignore Daddy but that question just seemed too big and long to answer at the moment.

"Mommy, are you sick?" Durinda asked.

"Of course not," Mommy said.

"Then why are you in bed?" Georgia said.

"Because of this," Mommy said, indicating the bundle in her arms. "I just had a baby."

A *baby?*

"But how?" Annie said.

"Where's the doctor?" Marcia said, looking all around the tower as though she expected to find a doctor hiding somewhere.

"Your father delivered it," Mommy said proudly.

"Oh, it was nothing," Daddy said. "It's amazing what you learn how to do when you're a model."

"Happy birthday, girls," Mommy said. "You didn't think I'd forget, did you?"

"Is that baby our present?" Georgia said.

"Well, it's the only thing I've got at the moment," Mommy said.

"I think I'd rather have a bike," Rebecca said.

"Is it a he baby or a she baby?" Jackie asked.

"A she baby," Daddy said.

"Oh," Jackie said. "Cute baby."

"Wait a second," Annie said. "Your sister"—and

here Annie paused, as though mustering the strength to say something — "*Aunt Queen* said she took you because you were trying to one-up her on something yet again. Is this baby that one-up?"

"Yes," Mommy said.

"Oh dear," Petal said. "I think I'm feeling a case of stupid sibling rivalry coming on."

"Ever since we were born," Mommy went on, "Queen has been intensely jealous of me because I was born a minute earlier than she was. She was intensely jealous even though she got the better first name."

"Oh, I don't know about that," Durinda said. "I think Lucy has its merits as a name too."

"Be that as it may," Mommy said, "Queen has always been intensely jealous. So when we turned eight and we got our powers — "

"Hang on," Georgia said. "You and Aunt Queen have powers too?"

"Of course," Mommy said. "All the people in my family who are going to get powers get them sometime in their eighth year. I assume you've all got yours now, don't you?"

Eight heads nodded.

"Daddy," Zinnia said, "did you know about Mommy's family and this power thing when you married her?"

Daddy nodded.

Zinnia stood on tiptoes so she could place her hand on his shoulder. "You are a brave man," she said.

"But what *are* your powers?" Georgia wanted to know.

"Well, Queen can obviously make people and objects smaller," Mommy said, "which is what she did to me starting when we turned eight. She'd make me smaller and then she'd shut me in her dollhouse. Do you realize that those dolls in dollhouses aren't the greatest conversationalists?"

We just looked at her.

"Anyway," Mommy went on, "all that sitting alone in the dollhouse just gave me more time to hone my own power, which only served to make Queen that much more jealous."

"But what *is* your power?" Marcia asked. "We've never seen you do anything magical."

"Why, my scientific mind and my inventions are my power," Mommy said, as if we should have known this all along.

Now we just looked at her some more.

"I hate to say this, Mommy, on our first day back together," Rebecca said, "but your inventions tend to stink."

"Excuse me?" Mommy said.

"What Rebecca means to say," Jackie said diplomatically, "is that they never quite work as one would think they might."

"Oh, really?" Mommy said. She cocked an eyebrow at us and we got the feeling that if she hadn't been holding that bundle of baby, she'd have folded her arms firmly in front of her chest. "For instance?"

"For instance," Rebecca said, "that flying watering can. It's supposed to water the plants, but it never really does it properly, so then we have to do it, and one time when I got mad about something it watered *me*."

"And that's a problem because . . . ?" Mommy said.

"Okay, then." Rebecca tried once more. "Maybe I deserved that. But what about robot Betty? She's supposed to be our housekeeper but she never does anything the way we ask her to. If we ask her to dust, she sits down at the desk."

"So who dusts?" Mommy said.

"We do," Rebecca said.

"And who does all the other chores when Betty fails to listen properly?"

"We do," Rebecca said.

We thought about that.

Oh.

*Oh!*

"I'd say my inventions are working out pretty well

so far," Mommy said, looking rather pleased with herself.

"About those inventions of yours, Mommy," Annie said. "Were you really working on the secret of eternal life? Because a few people have been asking about that."

"Oh no," Mommy groaned. "Was Serena one of them?"

"Yes," Annie said.

"Poor Serena," Mommy said. "She's always getting herself worked up about one thing or another. Her . . . *problems* all started when she turned eight and didn't get a power."

"She doesn't have a power?" Marcia said.

"No," Mommy said.

"Phew," Petal said, wiping her forehead.

"She's the only one in our family who doesn't," Mommy said.

"What about your brother," Annie asked, "our uncle George?"

"We went to his wedding to Aunt Martha this summer," Durinda added. "Did you know they were getting married?" Durinda hurried on, not waiting for an answer. "Anyway, he seemed nice enough and not at all evil, but I don't recall him having any powers."

"Funny," Mommy said, "I always forget about

George. No, he doesn't have any powers, and he doesn't know about Queen's and mine either. Somehow, we always managed to keep it from him. Anyway, not having a power has always made Serena very testy. But to answer your earlier question, no, I was never working on the secret of eternal life. That's just something I let people think to throw them off the scent of my really important experiments."

"Well, but," Annie said, "you're a member of SOLSA, the Secret of Life Scientific Agency, so you can't really blame people for what they think."

"That too," Mommy said.

"Wait a second," Rebecca said. "You've got one sister who does crazy things because she has no power, and you have a twin sister who takes you hostage because she thinks you're constantly trying to one-up her. Respectfully, Mommy, is everyone in your family nuts?"

Mommy considered this for a moment. "Yes," she finally said, "every last one, which is why I've been a little slow to introduce you to some of them."

A little slow?

"Respectfully," Rebecca asked in a softer voice, "are you nuts too, Mommy?"

Mommy considered this for an even longer moment. "I suppose I am," she finally said. Then she smiled. "But not in any way that's dangerous."

Phew.

"Not like Queen," Mommy went on. "She got a good education, and so did I. She married a handsome man, and so did I. Then we both had octuplets on the same day. You'd think she'd think our lives were pretty even. But no. As soon as she found out I was having a baby, a ninth baby, she took your father and me hostage so no one else would know I had something she didn't. But now that you all know, I'm sure she'll make us all regular size again and send us back to our world."

"About that," Annie said with a nervous smile. "Um, no. Now she says she plans to keep us all here."

Just then there was a soft tap at the tower door.

Who was that?

"It's Zinn," a voice whispered softly. "May I come in?"

"Are you alone?" Zinnia said, going to the door.

"Yes," Zinn whispered.

"All right then," Zinnia said, opening the door just wide enough to let him in and then quickly shutting it again.

Zinn looked at the bundle in Mommy's arms.

"Cute baby," he said. "Is that what this has all been about?"

We nodded.

He rolled his eyes. "Only Mummy would do this." He heaved a sigh. "Oh well. Never mind that now. We have more important things to discuss. Like, are you ready to get out of here now?"

"You want us to leave?" Zinnia said.

"Well." Rebecca sniffed. "I find this highly insulting."

"Actually," Petal said, "I would be happy to go any time now. I find this place spooky."

"It's not that I want you to leave," Zinn said, "but Mummy is getting a bit upset, so there's no telling what she'll do next. Plus, my brothers and I have talked it over and while we'd love for you to come visit again, we wouldn't want you to live here. It's too crowded. Plus, once you're safely out and the rest of the world knows about the baby, you'll no longer be in danger from Mummy, at least not over that. Plus, we'll get to go back to living in a normal-size house again and seeing other people. So as you can see, there are all kinds of pluses to go around."

"But how do we get out of here?" Marcia asked.

Zinn shrugged. "How did you get in?"

"Yes," Daddy said, "how did you ever get inside?"

So we explained about the infinity sign and the lying-down eight and all of us connecting ourselves to one another to make one giant symbol.

Zinn shrugged again. "If that's how you got in, it must be your way out."

"But there were exactly eight of us then," Georgia objected.

"And there are eleven now," Rebecca said. "I don't think we can make a figure eleven."

"No," Zinn said, "but you can make an eight with eleven. I don't think it's the number that counts so much as the shape."

Oh.

*Oh!*

"Are you sure it's okay for you and the baby to travel?" Durinda said as Mommy rose from the bed, bundle in her arms.

"We'll be fine," Mommy said.

"And I really should be getting home anyway," Daddy said. "The taxes are long overdue. I'm sure my accountant is having fits by now."

"Not to worry, Daddy," Annie said. "We took care of that. And we've taken care of paying all the bills too since you've been away."

We had a new respect for Annie in that moment. She could have said "I took care of that" and "I've taken care of paying all the bills," both of which would have been accurate. She *had* been the one to actually do those things. But instead, she'd given credit to all of us, and we realized that that was even more accurate. Because somehow, everything we'd done, we'd done together.

Well, except for the things each of us absolutely had to do on her own.

"Everybody ready?" Annie said, and we assumed our positions on the floor, forming a lying-down eight with eleven people, one of whom was the new baby held tightly in Mommy's arms.

"I hope you'll send notes," Zinnia said to Zinn, who gave us a little wave.

And then the earth shook, the sky spun, and it was all—

*Boom!*

*Bam!*

*Shazam!*

*Pow!*

*Kazowie!*

And, and, and—

# OUR FIRST EPILOGUE EVER

"Eights!" Pete shouted.

"Eights!" Mrs. Pete shouted.

"Eights!" the McG shouted.

"Eights!" the Mr. McG shouted.

"Eights!" Will Simms shouted.

"Eights!" Mandy Stenko shouted.

Yes, they were all still there.

"My," Daddy said, looking stunned as he helped Mommy to her feet, "this place is a little more crowded than I remember it being."

"Yes, well," Pete said, "we figured we'd better all wait until the Eights got back safely."

"How long would you have waited for us?" Jackie asked.

"Forever, if necessary, pet," Pete said, wiping a tear of joy from his eye. "Forever."

Oh, Pete.

We hugged him.

"Oh, and Mr. Huit?" Pete said. "I kept the Hummer in great shape for you while you were gone."

"Good man," Daddy said, clapping him on the back.

"Oh, and I also taught your oldest how to drive," Pete added, "accidentally."

Daddy raised a quizzical eyebrow at him.

"Perhaps I'd better explain how that came about," Pete said, and suddenly we were filling our parents in on everything that had happened since New Year's Eve, and then we were filling in the Petes, the McGs, Mandy, and Will on everything that had transpired in the snow globe.

"I can't *believe* you," Will said. "You Eights are *amazing!* And now there are *nine* of you! You're the Eights . . . plus one!"

Yes. That would take some getting used to.

"You mean," Mandy said to Mommy with a gulp, "that from now on, they'll have these powers all the time?"

"Well, yes," Mommy said, "but I'm sure they'll only use them when absolutely necessary and for the greater good."

We put on our best innocent faces, hoping everyone would believe her.

"And never during school hours," the McG said sternly.

"Unless absolutely necessary," the Mr. McG said. "You know, for the greater good."

Just then the cats made their presence known with much great meowing, so we acknowledged their presence with many good scratches under each chin.

"I feel cheated," Zinnia said glumly.

"How come, dear?" Mommy said.

"Because the other seven got a whole month when they were the center of attention," Zinnia said, "while I only got a measly week. Okay, eight days."

"Are you kidding me?" Rebecca said. "How self-centered can you get?"

Rebecca? Talking about someone else being self-centered?

She must have sensed our glares because she glared back at us. "What?" she said. "Just look at this day Zinnia's had, that we've all had—we've lived through an entire huge adventure in a single day!"

We hated to say the words but: *Rebecca was right.* It had been an amazing day.

"Is it still our birthday?" Georgia asked.

"Yes," Daddy said. "It's exactly eleven thirty at night."

"Eleven thirty?" Petal yawned. "No wonder I'm so tired."

"Could we open our presents now?" Zinnia said.

"Or at least eat our birthday cake?" Durinda said.

But we didn't get to do that right then because the doorbell rang.

We couldn't be absolutely certain but we were fairly certain no good could come from a ringing doorbell at eleven thirty at night.

"I'll get it," Mommy said, the bundle still in her arms.

It really was amazing, we thought, Mommy's energy level, considering she'd just had a baby that day.

We all trooped after Mommy toward the front door.

"Why," Daddy asked as we passed the front parlor, "is the suit of armor wearing my smoking jacket?"

"So he looks appropriate with that corncob pipe and your fedora," Annie said.

"Oh, I see," Daddy said.

Mommy opened the door, and we looked over her shoulder and saw who'd rung our doorbell. It was our evil toadstool of a next-door neighbor, the Wicket. She didn't have an evil fruitcake in her hands this time, but still.

"Can I help you?" Mommy said sweetly.

"You?" The Wicket squinted up at Mommy. "I wasn't expecting you. You're back?"

"Apparently," Mommy said.

"Well, never mind that now," the Wicket said. "I came because one of your girls is a witch."

"Are you joking?" Mommy said.

"I never joke," the Wicket said. "I saw her with my own eyes. She summoned animals to your front lawn and then she sent them all away. It was . . ." The Wicket's accusing finger scanned over all of us until finally settling on Zinnia. "That one!"

Poor Zinnia. The Wicket was forever getting our names wrong, but when you are distinctly the smallest it is easy to get pointed out in a crowd.

But what did this mean, Zinnia accused of being a witch?

Petal threw herself at the Wicket's ankles and held on tightly. "Please don't burn Zinnia at the stake," she begged. "She's one of the nicest to me and she takes up the least amount of space."

"Zinnia? A witch?" Mommy laughed. "Don't be ridiculous. Didn't you read about it in the newspaper?"

"Read about what?" the Wicket said.

"A few animals escaped from the zoo, but everything's fine now," Mommy said. "Now then, instead of accusing one of my children of being a witch, wouldn't you rather meet my new baby?"

"Oh no," the Wicket said. "You mean there's another one?"

For the first time, it really hit us. There *was* another one of us now, a little one, and what would this one be able to do when she hit eight?

Oh, this was a lot to get used to.

"See how beautiful she is?" Mommy said, holding the baby forward so the Wicket could get a better look whether she wanted to or not. "And you know what her father and I have decided to call her?"

We wanted to hear this too. Suddenly, we were dying to know.

"Nine," Mommy said, beaming.

"*Nein?*" the Wicket said. "The German word for 'no'? You've named your baby No?"

"No," Mommy said. "I mean, of course we didn't do that."

"Then you're calling her Nine?" the Wicket said. "Like the number?"

"Yes, like the number," Mommy said, "only we're going to spell it numerically, so she'll be 9." Mommy used one hand to trace the invisible number in the air. "Her name is 9 Huit. You see, Robert and I named the other girls with letters, starting with *A* and ending with *Z*. We thought if we gave the new baby a name using some random letter, she'd just feel like an afterthought. But this way, she'll feel extra special."

"This," the Wicket said, backing away, "is just the nuttiest house."

"I'll have Jackie bring over a piece of birthday cake tomorrow," Mommy called after the Wicket, "if there's any left. Hope you don't mind that it's not fruitcake!"

Then Mommy slammed the door.

* * * * * * * *

After we lit the candles, sang to each other, blew out the candles, and cut up the cake, we all sat around the table to eat it and to knock back a few juice boxes.

Mmm, mango—finally, not that unexotic starfruit again.

It was hard, as we ate, to keep our eyes off 9. We had a little sister! What would she be like? *Who* would she be like?

"Mmm," Rebecca said around a mouthful of cake, "good frosting."

Well, *some* of us couldn't take our eyes off 9.

"When you think about it," Jackie said, "this is like the Return with the Elixir."

"What's Jackie talking about?" Georgia said.

"Don't you remember my telling you about this once before?" Jackie said.

Georgia shook her head.

"It's from the book I read on screenwriting once," Jackie said. "Remember, in your month, when you sent away your gift I told you that you were refusing the Call to Adventure?"

"I think I vaguely remember something like that," Georgia admitted.

"Well, this is what happens at the end of the adventure," Jackie said. "If a heroine's journey is complete, she returns home with an elixir, which is really just some sort of good thing that's objective proof the journey has been a success."

"So 9's our elixir," Annie said.

"Yes," Jackie said, "I think so."

That was good. It was good to think of 9 that way, rather than as . . . *competition.*

"Oh, but I am depressed," Rebecca said, shocking us by putting her fork down while there was still frosting left on her piece of cake.

"Me too," Georgia said. "We have our elixir, so our journey has ended."

"No offense, Mommy and Daddy," Annie said, "we missed you horribly, but . . ."

"But when you were away, we were important," Durinda said.

"There was magic," Jackie said.

"Even if it was sometimes scary," Petal said.

"And great mysteries to solve," Zinnia said.

"Even if that was scary too," Petal said.

"But who are we now," Marcia said, "now that the adventures are over and the mysteries are as solved as mysteries can ever be solved?"

"You must be joking!" Will Simms said.

"You're going to be in fourth grade in just a few weeks," the McG said.

"A whole new grade," the Mr. McG said. "With maybe even a new teacher."

"You have a new baby in the house," Mrs. Pete said.

"Plus," Mommy said, "there'll always be some danger in your lives."

"How so?" Marcia asked.

"She means because of our powers," Annie said, proving once again that she could be as smart as an adult. "It's fine for people in this room to know about us, but if the greater world ever found out . . ."

She let that hang there in midthought, but even the dimmest among us could complete it easily enough. If word got out, other people, some of them even scientists but not at all like Mommy, would want to put us in a lab and study us. Governments and armies and all sorts of people would want us as secret weapons. Our lives would no longer be our own.

We gulped.

Our lives were good lives, and we couldn't, *wouldn't,* allow that to ever change.

"Plus, never mind all that," Pete said. "You're *you.*"

What did he mean by that? we wondered. We only hoped it wasn't an insult, not from Pete.

"What do you mean by that?" Mandy Stenko said, saving us from having to reveal our own heightened paranoia.

"He *means,*" Will said, "that *you* bring the mystery and magic and adventure with you. Because wherever you go, whatever you do, and even if there's now a 9, you're *the Eights!* So as long as you're around, the mystery and the magic and the adventure can never end."

Eight faces grinned from ear to ear.

And, in that moment, it was enough.

But wait a second. Wait just one second.

What was that mango juice box doing in 9's tiny hand, and how had it gotten there?

We all stared down at 9, shocked, as 9 looked back at us and giggled.

"Oh no," Daddy said. "We're going to need a bigger house."

# A LETTER TO READERS

If you're reading this note, you've finished reading *The Sisters Eight Book 9: The Final Battle . . . for Now.* I hope you liked it!

It's hard for me to believe how much time has passed since Greg, Jackie, and I started work on this series. For the public, the first book appeared in December 2008. But for us, it all started two years earlier. Jackie was six in December 2006 and we were staying with friends in Crested Butte, Colorado, when a snowstorm hit and the airport was closed. We were originally meant to stay there for six days, but the snowstorm kept us there for ten. There were no other kids in the area and our friends didn't have TV, so by the last few days we were looking for new ways to entertain ourselves. What would you do in such a situation? What we did was to begin brainstorming a book about eight sisters—octuplets—whose parents disappear one New Year's Eve. Jackie came up with names for the sisters, I named the cats, Greg contributed the crazy inventions such as flying watering cans, and we were off and running. Jackie also came up with all the powers and gifts for the Eights. At the time, it seemed cool that Zinnia's gift would be a snow globe—but who could have ever guessed that what seemed to be such a random choice on Jackie's part would turn out to play such a major role in the conclusion of the series?

We kept brainstorming as we flew home finally on Christmas Day, and when we got back to Danbury, Connecticut, I began writing, with Greg and Jackie providing ideas and input all the way through. At this point, it was still just to entertain ourselves—since we'd had so much fun dreaming up ideas for the story, we thought it would be fun just to see what the written book would be like. But then, once we were finished with that stage, we started thinking that maybe others would enjoy our creation as well, so I sent Book 1 off to my favorite editor in the world: Julia Richardson at Houghton Mifflin Harcourt, who agreed that people like you might like what we'd done.

As I write this letter, it's nearly five years since this all started. Five years! Jackie is eleven now and several inches taller than I am. Greg was always taller than I am. Oh, and we have a cat now too, Yoyo. Whenever Yoyo sees me writing here, he looks sure I must be writing about him.

I'd like to take this opportunity to thank some of the people who have helped the Sisters Eight series be what it is. Thank you to Lisa K. Weber, the artist who does the covers and interior illustrations for the books — we've never met Lisa, but no one else could have done a better job at visually representing what was born in our imaginations. Thank you to Carol Chu for design and lettering. Thank you to Karen Walsh for publicizing, Linda Magram for marketing, Betsy Groban for publishing, everyone else at HMH for doing everything else they do, and thank you to Julia, always Julia.

Most of all, though, I'd like to thank you. I've had twenty-two books published so far in my writing career, but nothing — *nothing* — has given me more joy than writing this with my family for you. And many of you have been writing too. We've received letters — oh, have we received letters! Mostly the letters come from kids, but they also come from parents, grandparents, teachers, librarians, booksellers. Often, you want to know when the next book will be out. But you also write to say that you're our "number 1 fan!" or that your family reads our books when you go on camping trips — often those come from the Canadian contingent. You send pictures of yourselves reading the books and pictures of Sisters Eight board games you've created. You send eleven-foot illustrated scrolls detailing your love for the series. Sometimes, you write or someone who loves you writes to say that you didn't like to read until you discovered the Sisters Eight. You have no idea what that means to a writer.

Your letters — we have saved them all.

Because of the love you've shown for the Sisters Eight from the very beginning, you have always been in my mind and heart as I write the words in each book. When I wrote the cliffhanger ending for *Book 4: Jackie's Jokes* and all those carrier pigeons thundered against the Huit home, each carrier pigeon delivering a note that said *Beware the Other Eights,* I hoped you would be left openmouthed. Whenever I had Rebecca say "Or else they're dead," I hoped that rather than being scared, you laughed, understanding how outrageously awful Rebecca can be. And when I wrote the last words of *Book 9: The Final Battle . . . for Now,* I hoped you would understand that even though all the major mysteries in the series have been resolved—what happened to the parents, who the Other Eights are, who the note leaver is, and so on—the door has been left open for future adventures, even if those adventures may only ever live in your imaginations and mine.

Thank you, once more, for all the joy you've given me.

So this is goodbye . . . for now! I'm off to write more books, and you're off to . . .

Where *are* you off to?

Oh, that's right. I'll tell you. You're off to keep being great readers of books and you're off to work hard in school because that's the best way for you to take over the world.

Thank you, thank you, forever thank you.

Lauren (and Greg and Jackie too!)

P.S. If you ever need me, you can always e-mail me through the contact link at www.laurenbaratzlogsted. com. As those of you who have written already know, I always write back.